"At turns unsettling and inspirational, *Pipette* tracks the lengths one woman must go to keep herself healthy, sane, and safe. When the narrator moves out of her boyfriend's home because of threatening behavior, she must grapple with not only rebuilding a home for herself but also with the resurfacing of troubling memories from her past, memories of playing nice to stay safe. As the COVID-19 pandemic advances, the narrator, a writer and English professor, takes a temporary job as a lab technician analyzing test results, finding satisfaction and even pleasure in the precision of her pipetting skills. A tool used to transfer measured liquids safely and accurately, the pipette might also serve as metaphor for how the narrator calibrates her daily activities, parceling the day into writing, self-care, and grueling exercise routines, ever pushing the limits of her body. 'I study variations of my heart rate,' she says. The pipette is also an apt metaphor for Chinquee's prose—sharp, precise chapters, each with the compression and satisfaction of a flash fiction. A moving novel of crystalline structure."
—Eva Heisler, author of *Reading Emily Dickinson in Icelandic*

"This extraordinary novel tells the story of a woman's ordinary days, lived under the twin shadows of war and the Covid-19 pandemic. In elegantly compressed prose, each short chapter opens a window onto an event or encounter. Sometimes we barely glimpse these moments, seen as if from a passing train. Sometimes the window widens into a door and we're invited inside: kitchen, bedroom, night streets, park. The narrator meditates on time passing, on life and death and meaning, all while focused on the details of each day. Here she is, massaging kale for salad. Here she is, missing her puppy during a workout. Here she is, in bed with a man who kisses her softly, then leaves the next day. Here she is, buying scrubs for a job at a Covid testing center, which brings back memories of time in the military, of faraway family, of the sickness

that hovers everywhere at once. What a gorgeous book, full of believable and urgent details that capture this moment with wisdom and precision. Understated and generous, Kim Chinquee's beautiful debut novel is a delight to read."
—Carol Guess, author of *Girl Zoo* and *Sleep Tight Satellite*

"Pipette is Kim Chinquee's novel of a fifty-something single woman navigating the life challenges of relationships, career and family history in the age of COVID.

Chinquee, a rock star in the flash fiction world, has published several award-winning collections of flash fiction. The chapters in this novel are flash-like in length and they propel the reader through the story, like scrolling through a Tik Tok feed. It's hard to put down.

Her prose is spare and clean and the narrative voice is dispassionate, which only makes the story more dramatic, more powerful, more heartbreaking, and ultimately more uplifting.

It is the story of a woman who does not let her fears control her life. It is a story of courage and triumph. Highly recommended."
—Len Joy-author of *Dry Heat* and *Casualties and Survivors*

"What makes a life and gives it meaning? In *Pipette*, Kim Chinquee explores this question through a hypnotic examination of daily rituals: how we care for the body, the self, and others; our behaviors as friends, lovers, and consumers. Like a lid of ice over a lake, these everyday acts support us through triumph and tragedy. But when the Covid pandemic shatters the world and its surfaces, Chinquee shows the reader in deft and compelling language that sometimes diving far into the depths is the only path to survival."
—Emma Bolden, author of *The Tiger and the Cage*

"In her new book, Kim Chinquee deftly explores the possible ranges of meaning that can grow out of the declarative. Frequently,

we are invited to examine her speaker caught in her own rut, drawn in the prosaic domestic. But these pieces are more than mere portraiture; instead, they are expert studies in the range of significance that arises from a single moment, no matter its seeming insignificance. This is an author who knows how to take nothing for granted!"
—Kyle McCord, author of *Reunion of the Good Weather Suicide Cult*

"Chinquee's novella is a bold exercise in form--urgent and experimental yet easy to understand and eminently enjoyable. There is a simplicity to her prose, much of it is pared back and precise. It takes some skill to write so sparingly and requires a self-confidence born from experience and commitment to the craft of writing. Chinquee is a clever writer who is always in control of her material. It's no surprise that her previous work has been nominated for numerous prizes and published in a variety of well-respected literary journals.

IR Verdict: Kim Chinquee's *Pipette* is an inventive and intelligent novella with writing so spare and carefully considered that not a word is wasted. A gem of a book."
—IndieReader, indiereader.com

Read more at http://www.kimchinquee.com

PIPETTE
by Kim Chinquee

a novel

Pipette starts with a woman on a train
returning from the ballet, to her dogs, her partner.
Then things escalate.

Also by Kim Chinquee

Oh Baby
Pretty
Pistol
Veer
Shot Girls
Wetsuit
Snowdog

Cover design: Joan Wilking

Copyright©2022 Kim Chinquee

ISBN: 978-1-7369169-0-2
LCCN: 2022946184

First Edition

Published by Ravenna Press
ravennapress.com

to Geneva

BALLERINA

At the ballet, a strong man carries with grace his ballerina. They're beautiful, in their green and white tights. They do pirouettes.

I have dreams of pipetting in the heavens, and when I wake, the bed is small and hard. The walls are cinder. I'm at the Y. I sleep in the same clothes I wore on the train over.

I get back on the train. It's a long way home.

The man in blue continues to be the man in blue. The men in blue take tickets. The train stops. It makes a whistle. The horn, it whooshes and whirls.

I PET AS MANY AS I CAN

It's not like my dogs are not OK, but it's not like having children. My son is an adult now with dogs and a wife.

I was staying at the Y, near Central Park, and spent a good deal of my time with men. We brushed our teeth in the same sink. We bathed, using the same water. We sometimes relieved ourselves without shutting the doors.

I also petted as many dogs on leashes as I could. All the dogs seemed very interested in me.

I drive my car an hour after the train ride. When I get to the door, the dogs greet me, helicoptering around.

I guess I'm just kind of a doggy lady.

SERVING IN THE TROPICS

Speak to me, I say to my dog Pip.

He barks.

I make kale chips, blending cashews in the blender with oil and garlic. I knead the greens.

As I quiet my device, the Spanish music from the next room voices a crescendo.

I used to make baby food in the blender, juice in the juicer, saving the pulp for muffins.

I say to Pip, No news, please. His head cocks.

The president talks of war. I served in a war. I was a medic. I collected blood. I used to pipette.

My son's serving in the tropics. There are pictures of him with ammunition strung across his body like a sash. There are videos of him and his soldiers in their night gear, goggles. I can hear their breaths, the sounds of their boots. He lifts weights. I picture him at night with his dog, his one-eyed kitten. I picture myself with him so little, after a C-section delivery because he was losing oxygen.

I taste the batter, add more salt.

I add the mixture to the kale.

Pip, he sits and waits. His eyes are wide.

SPINNING THE WHEELS

During my run, I play Pandora. Hook up the earbuds my son gave me a couple years ago for Christmas. I used to run with him in the jogger when he was a toddler and I was stationed in England in the air force. I had a bulky CD player that I could attach to my arm. I played tunes by The Cars, Wilson Phillips, Depeche Mode. I pushed my son, spinning the wheels, through the paths in fields, up hills. Through the town of Bourton-on-the-Water, past buildings of stone, a deer farm, and fields of purple, green and gold. There was a bumpy bridge that made him laugh, where he'd put his arms up. He was in diapers. I'd left his dad.

Today my Pandora plays Max Richter. I'm back in training. When I told my son, he said he was proud. He sent me gloves. I was proud that he was proud, proud that he'd thought to send me a gift.

I create a story while I run. The sounds become colors. The colors become tastes. The tastes become a tingling in my body. My body floats. I remember the ballet I attended days before. My body is a dancer. I run along the shoulder of a highway. Cars pass, buzzing. Snow covers fields. Trees stand bare and cold. Cows stir into a barn and out again. I saw the *Nutcracker Suite*. The cows are Holsteins. They remind me of my childhood.

I become electric. I can be up and down and around. I get high and it's hard for me to describe it.

Once home, I take off my clothes and I put them in the washer. My partner Henry's just home from his bike ride and his clothes are caked with mud.

After I'm showered and in sweats, I find Henry's workout posted on Strava, the app we each have on our phones. I join him in this sinkhole: seeing all kinds of athletes on the app who are his friends and maybe also mine. Serial friends. I even find my son there. He's been running.

I first connected with Henry though Facebook nine years ago because we had so many mutual athlete friends there. We hooked up. We ran. We dated. We broke up. We got back together.

I buy his groceries. We wake up. We love each other. We watch movies. We drink coffee. We fuck. I get on his nerves sometimes. He walks the dogs. I walk them too. They hog the bed.

His parents send me texts. His sister loves me. He has ugly toes. And here, now he's on the bed, looking into his phone, probably on Strava, and I think maybe he's simply avoiding me, or maybe even wants to find another girl there.

It's just an app. Making us dinner, I heat up the burner, add oil to the pan. Add an onion, garlic, ginger. Turn on the overhead fan.

HOW TO BE

Turn it up, I say to my guide. She's a hypnotherapist who uses acupressure. For the past decade she's lived in California. Buffalo is a shock to her, with its wings and beer and climate.

I'm not from here either. My first time in Buffalo was many years ago to read flash fiction at a gallery with a leak in the roof. I came for the job here some years later.

She's a short woman, but seems large and wise in her soul, in her voice and in the ways she directs me. She wears long scarves and large-framed glasses. Her hair is a mix of brown and grey.

We recap our last session.

I'm better, I say. I used the technique from last time. Pressing my thumb to my index finger, imagining my father accepting me, telling me he's sorry. My father is dead. My guide sends me to his spirit. He was schizophrenic. He didn't know how to be.

I take off my shoes and lay back on the table. As I close my eyes and she counts and talks, she takes me back to my former counselor who last week jumped from a high rise. She brings me back to my father. I imagine them in the sky playing cards. My dad played card games when he was alive. My late counselor once gave me a card that said I'm not responsible for anyone else's feelings.

I went to a retreat last summer. The place felt to me like healing—good and healthy food. No vehicles on site. Quiet. Gardens. Without phones. I spent a whole week in meditation, relaxing my ego. I'd taken a train. Henry had just threatened to kick me out again. So I let it sit. I wait to let things happen.

That's how I found my guide. My eyes are closed and I'm going back into my deepest parts. Two and three, and deeper five and six. My guide touches my feet. I imagine a man in a beret. Wearing earbuds. He turns the music up—I'm here but not here, like I'm erased. Seven and eight and nine. I'm drinking Kombucha and something isn't dandy. Ten and… eleven, who am I?

THE DISTANCE BETWEEN MYSELF

Dive right in, says the ski instructor as we board the magic carpet.

I picture a lagoon below as the carpet takes us higher. It's a belt, like the escalator I used to be afraid of at the mall. Once, when I was small, shopping with my mom and sister, they went up without me. I stood at the bottom, looking up and crying. Finally a stranger lifted me and put me on the stair and told me to hold onto the handrail.

As we go up, bulbed heads go down the mini ski slope. Mostly children. Some on snowboards, some on skis. Some parents ski backwards, guiding their kids along.

I drive by these slopes each day. Can see the lights at night when I walk the dogs in the neighborhood. I can hear laughter, the swoosh and whoosh, sometimes music on the speakers. From the road, it looks like a laboratory of fun I long to be a part of.

This isn't my first lesson. Last year, I had three. I've lived in this neighborhood two years, with Henry, who used to do the slalom race in college, was on ski patrol, and traveled to the Alps when he was a kid. When he skis, he makes it look easy. All I have do is see the ledge and I picture myself a smashed tomato. Tomatillo. Plum.

I bought a season pass this year that comes with free ski lessons.

Pizza, pizza! French fry, the instructor says, referring to the way I should angle my skis. I spend more energy trying to get myself up from falling than when I stay upright.

After yet another fall, the instructor grabs my arm and helps me. He says, You're shaking.

I'm terrified! I say.

It's supposed to be a group lesson. I'm the only one who showed. After I finally spend some time not falling, the instructor takes me to the "regular" lift, and as we ride the chair, I look below, measuring the distance between myself and what's below. As the lift approaches the place where we get off, I fall right away. My instructor is older—probably older than my dad if he were alive. I keep having to stop because I see the drops and trees and get scared when I go faster. After a while, I ask if I can take my skis off and just walk down the rest of the way.

I bend my legs. They're sore from running. Sore from swimming. Sore from biking. I'm a triathlete. I grew up a farm girl, afraid of falling from the hayloft. I'm 51. If only I could ski.

To the right of me is a big wide ledge that goes straight down to the highway. I breathe. I look ahead.

Dive in! says the instructor.

I look at him. My hands shake.

SWAT TEAM

A swat team was brought in, I hear from the TV. Henry keeps the channel on the news. I'm in the kitchen, making more kale chips. I wash the dishes, dry them. I shout out to Henry, Need anything?

He joins me, gets out the cutting board, slices up a turnip. He says, Only you.

The knife makes a hard sound against the board. The TV blares something loud about a blowup. Our dogs stand at our feet. They wait for something to drop.

POP

I ask Henry to wash his hands. You can't share your utensils with the dogs, I say.

After he and I reunited, four years after we broke up, we met up at the park.

It was nice to see him after all that time. I missed the way he touched me. The way we lay together after making love with the rain on the roof.

Our dogs circle around the coffee table. His two and my two.

They jump and they pop.

A MEAN ROAR

My new Vitamix arrives in the mail. When I take it out of the box, I can hardly believe it.

It's the same Pro 750 that I bought at the Williams Sonoma eight years before. It cost me, at that time, a lot, but I didn't care about that. It does things like make soup and peanut butter. Chop up greens so they don't seem like greens anymore. The machine has a mean roar. I probably didn't treat my first machine properly. Letting things sit in the blender. The insides of it broke. After I called headquarters, they said my warranty had expired, but I could still get a rebate.

I wrapped it up. Sent it off.

After the new one's out of the box, I set it up. Take pictures.

I like machines. It's like my days of working in the lab. Where I learned to pipette.

KINK IT UP

One more time, says the voice from the TV. I'm on the sofa, trying to read, and Henry tilts his feet at an angle in front of him. He faces the TV. The man on the TV says, Exhale.

Henry gets down on his knees, puts his arms in front of him, and lowers his butt. He looks a little silly.

Outside the snow has melted, so there's no skiing for us today. No fat biking on the trails behind our house, no snowshoeing for us, either. And the gym is closed, because of a power outage. I told Henry, We can always run. But he's not so much into running anymore, not like the days when we were new. He was fast, back then, faster than me, and then he got Achilles tendonitis. Now he mostly mountain bikes and fat bikes, going up big hills and around ledges, between trees, over roots and stones. Sometimes I go with him, but it scares me. I'm still mostly into running—but I'm not as fast as I used to be either. I swim a lot at the gym. Then sweat in the steam room and hot tub. I may run later. But I'm sore from yesterday's run—I ran to the next town, on the highway. Today, I may finish this book, hang out with our dogs and watch Henry.

He's wearing corduroy pants and a button-up top that's a little too small for him. He raises his butt like the man in the video.

In this book, I read an essay about folks who frequent an app called Second Life, where they can create an avatar and find a partner, choose kids and buy boats and condos. It sounds confusing, but I'm still early into the essay. To spend hours on a computer with a second life—how would that feel, in the body?

The man on the video says, Twist your neck, and Henry's standing now, with his neck kinked, his head touching his left shoulder.

I could be doing the video with him, I suppose. I'm not into any physical workout that speaks to me from a voice on the TV.

Kink it up! I say to Henry. He's breathing heavy. My book is a hardcover. I hold it on my lap. I like the feel of the pages, marking up words and phrases with my Moleskin pen. Sometimes I fold corners.

Kink it, says the man on the TV again.

Kinky, I say.

Henry stands. He turns to me and flashes me the finger.

JOKER

In the living room, Henry's watching *Joker*. Joker laughs. Joaquin Phoenix doesn't look like Joaquin Phoenix. Wow, I say, that's some really good acting.

The movie's halfway over.

Like most nights, Raven's on the loveseat on her back with her legs out, and her head curled behind her. Henry calls it her ballet.

Pip's on the top of the sofa, behind Henry; Happy, with his head on Henry's lap, snores.

Bird, of course, is reserving her place on the bed. I go there, pulling back the covers.

Bird, I say, you have to move over.

Honey, Henry shouts from the living room. You have to finish *Joker*!

My eyelids are so heavy.

He says, You have to see.

I go back to the living room. Henry's rubbing his shoulder where he hurt it last year mountain biking, falling on a rock.

I say, How you feeling?

He says, Kind of jokey.

He laughs like Joker. He gets up and dances and points to the screen.

QUIET, PLEASE

Quiet, please, I say to the dogs. They're going nuts again. Henry's just taken them out for their morning walk, and now he's wheeling the garbage bin to the end of the driveway.

This battery of morning activity is usual: the dogs crawl over us, either Henry (or both of us) get up, we scoop the dog food into the corresponding dishes: Raven in the bathroom, Happy in the bedroom, Bird and Pip in the kitchen. While they're eating, Henry will do his business in the bathroom. I'll start up his breakfast, putting water in a saucepan, oatmeal, chia seeds, honey, cinnamon, turn it up, then add blueberries and half of a banana. Throw out yesterday's coffee filter, add a new one and new grounds, dump water where it belongs. I'll toast some sprouted grain bread for myself, stir the pot, and once the toaster beeps, I'll find a knife, if I can find a clean one, add the organic peanut butter (without sugar), then raw local honey. I'll hear the coffee percolate, watch the colors in the saucepan kaleidoscope: the blueberries bleeding into the oatmeal. I'll add walnuts for texture. Bird will probably paw at her dish, asking for more water, and Pip will look up at me. I'll eat my toast standing up. Pour myself some coffee, and then Henry will come out of the bathroom, Raven following and looking for more food. One of us will open the bedroom door, and Happy will emerge, his body wobbling like a slinky, and he'll sniff around. I'll offer a bite of my toast to Henry and he'll take a big one. He'll head downstairs and the dogs will follow, maybe run ahead of him, save maybe Happy, who is desperate for any food that's fallen. He'll sniff around. Dogs will run in circles, thumping and maybe running up the stairs again, then down. Pip will bark and probably wait on the back of the basement's big brown sofa.

Henry will gather up the leashes that hang from the thing on the wall he nailed near the door. He'll have poop bags in his pocket. He'll tell them to sit. The leashes make clinging sounds: Raven and Bird are assigned choke collars, which, I hope, don't ever actually choke them. Bird's leash has a belt that wraps around the person walking. She knows how to escape. If (or rather when) she does, she'll sprint around the neighborhood for hours, playing her game of getting close but not too close for anyone to catch her. She'll jump over sticks, do a slalom through the trees, into creeks and ponds and other people's driveways. Once, when I tried to catch her in my car, she followed me over a mile down the highway, to the Pizza Glen, and when someone there opened the door, she ran right in, to the back of the kitchen.

Once the dogs are leashed, Henry, after putting on his own gear, will take them out, and I'll hear the door shut. I'll log onto my computer, check my email, bank account. I'll brush my teeth. I'll look in the mirror, and decide whether, today, I'll wear my glasses or my contacts.

He's back now. Wheeling the garbage tote down the driveway. Today is windy, with new snow on the ground. Branches wave. The sides of this house are made up of tall windows.

Sometimes, after Henry walks the dogs, he'll fold the laundry he may have put, the night before, in the dryer.

He comes up the stairs with a stack full of clothes.

He's wearing just his swim trunks. He says, Which way to the beach?

CONTROL THE ROOM

Henry's back at it again: feet in the air, hands on his raised back, shoulders pressed to the mat. The guy on the TV says, Control the room, and as the people on the screen unroll their bodies, so does Henry. Now he's on his butt, touching his right elbow to his left knee.

The instructor says, Keep your spine straight. Release. Left hand, now. Deep breath. Exhale.

The dogs surround him. Bird chews her lamb toy that's turned brown and ragged. Raven watches from the loveseat. I'm at my computer, writing my flash fiction.

Henry's on his hands and knees now. The guy on TV is on his back and Henry turns over. They're doing something with their tummies. Egg rolls. Molding their bodies.

Yesterday, Henry went skiing with the little snow that was left on the slopes. I went to get my hair done, where my stylist talked about her detox from pot. I went grocery shopping. Took back *Joker*. Came home with a headache I figured was from tension.

Henry said he weighed himself. He said to me, I'm fat.

I said to him, You're not. I took off his clothes and took him to the bedroom.

I took an ibuprofen. Made dinner. Went to bed.

Henry stands. Bird's on her back, tummy up. Raven's tail wags. Happy chews his squeak toy, and Pip watches him, watches me.

WHERE WE STAND

Three, two, one, says the man on the TV. The man by now is probably over sixty. The DVD is old. The man says to drive the elbows. I write at my computer while Henry squats like a centipede.

He wears the new slippers I bought him. Happy's always chewing up his old ones.

After Henry's done with his exercise, I sit with him on the sofa. The news is on. The impeachment.

He says, The dogs voted for Trump.

I say, Maybe yours did.

We both know where we stand. I'm liberal. He's a registered democrat, but, like a lot of voters, it doesn't mean he votes that.

I pet Happy. He's on his back with his paws up. His fur is soft. I wipe his eyes. He always looks like he's crying.

Henry watches the screen. I get up, making him a sandwich.

He eats it while I fidget in the kitchen. He's glued to Fox News.

I say, Can we change the channel?

He changes into his work clothes. I turn off the TV, then get Henry his magnetized name tag from the fridge door. I hand him his lunch. I make sure he has his phone. I hand him his agenda, his jacket, and kiss him goodbye.

Back at my computer, I read. My desk is stacked with books and papers. I start to think about the last time he kicked me out—it's his house: all the stuff there is to move. We were fighting about politics again—him making fun of liberals.

I took all the things from the walls. Took my artwork to my office on campus. That's an hour away. I made three trips, and then, when he changed his mind, took all those trips by myself to bring it all back again. I didn't know what else to do—move out? Could I afford it?

I think about finding somewhere else to live.

I hear the door shut and listen as he starts his Jeep. After some time has passed, I look out to be sure he's away.

OH, WHAT FUN

What time is it? I say to Henry every morning. I wear an eye mask and ear plugs. He's the one with the alarm. When I peek from behind my mask, I can gauge the time by the amount of light. We don't bother with blinds or curtains.

Sometimes the dogs wake before his alarm. And since I'm between semesters, the only things getting me up are Henry and the dogs. This morning, I wake with only one ear plug—so it goes. I usually end up taking them out sometime during the night and they end up on the floor, or under covers. Happy likes to eat them.

Henry says, Seven thirty. It's kind of late for his usual workday. By the time he walks the dogs, eats his breakfast while watching the news, changes his clothes and gathers his things, he'll be challenging the clock.

I hear a gross sound, and go to the bathroom, finding Raven's face leaning into the floor. I keep reminding Henry to stop sharing his food with her. He usually eats on the sofa in front of the TV. When we first moved here, I used to serve us at the table. But the table's full of stuff now. It's a really nice table, crafted by a local artist while my house was being built. Oh, what fun that was: picking everything out. Fixtures, moldings, floorings. The stone and the cement. I miss gardening. I planted vegetables and trees. I pruned them and fed them. I sold that home to move in with Henry.

I start making coffee, and say, I believe you gave her popcorn.

He worked last night until nine, so instead of dinner, I made popcorn. We watched a movie where a guy pretends to disappear. He hides in the carriage room facing the house and watches his wife and family go about without him.

While Henry walks the dogs, I go to my computer and reread the fiction I wrote the day before about a woman who runs away from family. I build a fire. I clean the tub and take a salt bath. I lounge in my pajamas, watching the snow fall and the wind blow. Branches wave and dance—the main room consists of mostly windows. It's like living in a snow globe.

My desk faces the fireplace and over the fireplace is the portrait of our dogs. I'd commissioned an artist I met in Vermont to paint it for Henry. I gave it to him after he kicked me out this last time. That was the week of Christmas.

I go to YouTube, where I binge-watch footage of koala bears escaping fires in Australia.

A GIANT SPACESHIP

Henry texts, saying he's at Tops. Is there anything we need?

I'm heading out for a run. It's after six, and dark. Cold. I'm wearing two pairs of leggings, three shirts, a jacket and a hooded, sleeveless coat. A hat, mittens, my neck gaiter, a reflective vest, a headlamp. My GPS, and my headphones.

Every step is dreadful. The roads are slushy, icy in some places. I can see my breath. My music—today Max Richter—lifts me; it blasts from my earbuds and echoes in my hood. The loop I usually do is 1.25 miles and hilly.

At the back end of the loop, and at its highest peak, I see lights from the ski slope across the highway. They glow like a giant spaceship. I imagine all the people there, having fun and laughing.

I stop to take a picture, thinking I'll post it once I download my run on Strava. I take a selfie. It doesn't turn out because my breath is in the way and my headlight is shining. So I turn off the light. My face is red.

GET IN, GET OUT

I'm at the restaurant, alone, trying to get in some writing. I order a salad. I came to Springville to get out of the house. I don't know anyone who lives here.

I'd asked Henry to buy me some Fresca on his way home from work last night, but instead he got me a generic grapefruit soda that isn't sugar-free. He told me, in a text, They haven't made Fresca since 1975. I like Fresca. It's refreshing. I've been drinking a lot more of that since I'm drinking less wine.

He brought home firewood. We made a fire. I made more popcorn. We watched another movie. This one was about a blind opera singer from Italy.

I'm on my computer at the restaurant. I can use their Wi-Fi. I order a Corona. It's a Mexican place I've been to before with Henry. There aren't many restaurants in Springville. There isn't much in Springville besides a Walmart and a Tops. A McDonald's,

Taco Bell, Burger King, Dunkin Donuts, a Rite Aid, a hospital, a few gas stations, a Tractor Supply. I might be the only liberal.

Henry used to work at a dealership here before he got fired again and started working at the one he's at now. There's a main drag with a few stoplights. One liquor store called Cheap Chollies. It's the closest town from our neighborhood.

There aren't really many people here at the restaurant. The waitresses are big and middle-aged. They bring me salsa and chips right away. I knew they'd bring salsa and chips right away.

I suppose that's all I need now.

WORDSCAPE

Henry's been doing so many workout DVDs lately that I'm starting to memorize the commands: Find your balance. Stretch it out. One more time. Exhale, inhale, exhale.

I even start making up my own commands: Bounce it out. Bacteria the clean stuff. Go to contest with your bargain.

I play a game called Wordscape, where I get letters and make them into as many words in a set time as I can: P, E, O, N, L, Y. Peony, peon, pony, lope, nope, yep, one. Open. Only is obvious.

Freeze the melted ice cube.

While Henry skis, I review my syllabi: verifying the accuracy of dates and comparing rubrics from previous semesters. I make a fire. Watch the pretty snowfall. Glad I'm not on the slope, probably breaking bones or at least worried I will.

Henry comes home happy and gifts me a Kissing Bridge T-shirt. I'm not sure why. It's a size small and I'm not a size small anymore.

I make him chicken and rice and warm the cauliflower soup I made in my Vitamix. The football games are on. Two quarters in, the Packers are losing. I'm from Green Bay. My last class reunion was at Lambeau Field. Henry was with me.

I take some sleeping pills. Go to bed.

BIRD

I ask Henry, Know what I do while you're gone?

Write?

Talk to our dogs.

He gives me his never-mind look.

I sit there petting Bird. She's been glued to me.

There are fireworks. The neighboring ski place has an anniversary. Raven barks. Bird hides under my desk. Happy goes to the basement. Pip sits on my lap.

There's a delicious layer of snow on the trees. On the ground. On my car. It's kind of buried.

The sun is out and before Henry leaves for work, he tells me I should try to get out to the slope for a lesson.

I might have a fever.

The sun starts to shine.

I say to the dogs, Look.

Bird is the first to pay attention. I go to her and cuddle her like I used to when she was a puppy.

A few days after I moved in, I came home to find blood on the stairs. Blood in the hallway. Blood in the kitchen. Furniture was pushed around, some knocked over. Happy and Pip were hiding. I found blood in the tub. Blood in the living room. I found Bird hiding under my desk. She looked up at me. Blood dripped from her head. She couldn't stand.

I started the car. I put Raven in her crate. Happy and Pip looked at me with their heads tilted.

I lifted Bird and carried her to my Mercedes.

It was one below zero. The driveway wasn't plowed yet.

My wheels spun on the driveway and my phone was dying. I had no GPS signal and was low on gas. Bird whined a little. She dripped. She looked kind of like a zombie.

Keep it simple, I say to the dogs.

That night Bird lost a lot of blood. She had anesthesia. Surgery. Henry wasn't there because he went home to clean.

Raven had attacked her.

Keep it simple, I say to myself. I say it all the time now.

MAY I REFRESH YOUR BEVERAGE?

Move closer, I say to the guy at the bar, so I can hear you.

We're at the club on campus where students studying hospitality serve affiliates: faculty, staff, alumni. Donors.

Classes start next week. I'm on campus for meetings.

The guy I'm talking with has bright red lips. Blonde hair. He always wears suits. He has the whitest teeth. He's about my age.

His eyes are a deep blue. He smiles when he talks. He says, Elle, how are you?

I sip Prosecco. The usuals are here: Ron from biology is growing his beard out. Stan from history serves on the board, does the iPad Tuesdays, and has his own chair. Angie from hospitality is always donned in her color-matched outfits. Amy, who works at the museum, is a budding comedian, and comes in with her jokes.

Kimmy, the bartender, has strong arms and is always smiling, asking, May I refresh your beverage?

The guy I sit with, Alex, is a director of film operations. Lately, for various reasons, a lot of films are being made here.

I say, What's the newest?

Across the bar are members from administration. I try to be collegial.

Alex looks at me and says, You look nice tonight. I like your new cut.

I smile at Kimmy, who pours me a fluff. I raise my glass to Alex, and he gives me a nod.

IMPEACH

Henry's out on his fat bike on his day off. I'm on my last days of freedom before going back to teach. Today I have to read some stories for an anthology, talk on the phone with fellow board members. Write. Read. Henry asked me to go out for a ride, but I told him I might have a virus.

The trees are heavy with snow, and icicles hang. The sun shines. We slept past nine today. Fell asleep before ten last night during a hockey movie Henry had chosen on Netflix. I had dreams that I lived in an airport and kept having to go through security while carrying a primrose. I woke up blind because I was wearing my eye mask.

I turn the TV to CNN, where Adam Schiff talks about impeachment. If Henry were here, we'd be watching something different. Politics produces arguments here.

We have lots of TVs. One is in an area downstairs that never gets used and has Henry's long sofa, a few of my chairs, his armoire.

There's a bar area that's mostly cluttered with his bike tools. Also, by the door is my big brown sofa. There's also a bathroom with a washer and dryer. A tub. Another room is full of skis. Snowshoes. Camping equipment. Weights. It houses our bikes. We have nine between us. At first, I pictured him watching one TV downstairs while I was upstairs at my desk.

One TV is in the guestroom downstairs which has mostly my books and art supplies and clothes that no longer fit me. I've been spending a lot more time there. It's where I sleep when we're fighting.

There's a patio door that goes from the living area to outside. It's kind of like a mud room. The house has a smell to it.

Henry calls to let me know he's still out riding. He's out of breath.

I'm still here, he says. The ice broke after I went over it.

Jesus, I say. I'm a little jealous of his fearlessness. I could be out there. I'd be scared. Probably cold. Probably falling through the ice again.

I tell Henry to have fun and be careful.

I go back to my work. Henry's mom texts me, asks if we can move our weekend brunch ahead an hour so she can go to Bible class. I say yes. She thanks the Lord. The dogs hang around. Raven stands on the loveseat and looks out the window with her ears perked. On TV, I hear words of corruption.

I DON'T HAVE TO GO DOWN

Henry's in a hurry, getting ready for work. Trying to find his favorite pants. I say, Have you looked inside the dresser?

He works through a stack. He's good at folding clothes, but not at remembering where he puts them. He can recite lines from movies and books he saw and read in college. He remembers his high school race times. But he might not remember that he's told me his winning times already. I used to think he was a bad listener. Eight months into our relationship, the first time, one day while he was at work, I found meds in the bathroom cabinet. I know what his meds are for. My dad was on them.

After I asked Henry about his medication, he said it wasn't something he felt a need to announce. He's been on them for years.

He gets his thrills by riding through the woods, over hills, through creeks and close to ledges.

On my way to campus, I drive by the slope, seeing figures look like cells under a scope. I don't see anyone falling, but I also don't have a lot of time to look. When I see that hill, I see every fear of mine mounted, like going to camp and having to canoe. Standing in front of a room full of people, when I was in 4-H and giving a speech about phobias: "the only thing we have to fear is fear itself."

CROSS-COUNTRY

Before leaving the house I tell Henry maybe I'll look into buying cross-country skis. I say, Maybe that'll help me with the downhill.

When I was in junior high, one of my best friends had cross-country skis and we took them out behind the school. I wasn't afraid. She was afraid of driving. Last year, while driving to the grocery, she was killed head-on. She'd just written me two days before that.

Henry says, Cross-country's a lot harder.

I say, But I don't have to go down slopes.

I proposed, over a year ago, we buy cross-country skis for each other for Christmas. But Henry's shoulder was still injured. And I'd recently had surgery. He reacted in a way that wasn't pleasant.

As I drive along the highway, I admire the steep hills, the arrangement of the snow and the sky and the land and the curves and lines, like a wild canvas. I'm here, safe on the road, imagining the ground beneath me, polished and smooth. I'm just a person in a car, driving it, like an antibody, in a shell, a giant loaded muscle.

SYNCOPE

It's a perfect day to ski, Henry says before he leaves for work.

I'm back in bed, falling in and out of sleep after making him breakfast. He leans in, kisses me and says he loves me. Be good, he says. No misbehaving.

It's past ten, and I get up, drinking coffee. The TV's on, airing the impeachment. Raven's still on the bed, Happy and Pip sit on the sofa, and Bird lies on the floor. Hey Petunia, I say to Bird, moving to my desk chair.

I put on my wool hat, the one with flaps to cover my ears.

I make a note of my chores: Write and read and answer emails. Call back my colleague, John. Do committee stuff. Edit. Prep.

Snow sits heavy on the trees, making their branches look weary. My plants need watering. They grow like monsters with big hands. Some of my plants didn't survive after they moved here.

I call John back and ask him how he is. He's just coming off sabbatical—he didn't have to teach last semester, but he still hung around, meeting me on campus.

What texts are you using?

Did you get my syllabus?

Oh yes! Thanks! He asks, What are you up to?

Writing. Home. The usual.

Will you be on campus?

I might have to ski.

He asks about cross-country, downhill, tells me he tried once and loved it.

I say, I'm not so graceful. I might have to pray.

I get up from my desk, feel faint, and hang onto the handrail. I recall last night, getting up too fast and hanging on to Henry. Syncope. I fell and hit my head once. I'd had it checked some time ago, had a tilt test and there was nothing wrong with me. I've been having episodes on and off since I was fifteen. It's odd, how easy I forget before having to remember.

John's still on the line.

Sorry. What? I say.

He says, But you're a rock star.

DOWNHILL

I'm at the ski rental place again. I sit on a bench, and a worker says, Lift your feet. I have my rental boots on and she's showing me how to clip into the skis—cross-country.

A tall fit guy, one of the owners, greets a couple probably in their twenties. They talk about skiing in Colorado, a date in the Alps. Most of the clients here go downhill. I ask the woman helping me, Will this help me get better on the downhill?

Two small boys are running around. One is eating an orange. The woman helping me says, It's about the math. A man next to her says, An optical illusion.

Suddenly the whole place is packed with people. I can barely move my arms. And everyone, every single person except me, is carrying a pickle.

TREAT

In front of the TV, Henry lunges on the mat and grabs his right ankle. He wears slippers. Happy chews his squeak toy. The instructor from the TV talks about happier lives. Raven stands by the loveseat, near Henry, resting her chin on the cushion. Bird sits at my feet, her front paws out, and Pip is on the top of the sofa, head tilted. I say, Treat?.

Henry follows the commands. Bird gets behind the sofa and Happy nips his toy. Pip gets up and starts humping Happy. Raven hops on the loveseat.

Later we have brunch with Henry's parents at a place called Iron Kettle. Henry gets his usual two by two, which includes eggs and French toast and some bacon; his dad Bill gets something similar, and his mom Marylou orders the veggie omelet, which she gets every time and raves about how good it is, how filling! With spinach and cheese and broccoli and mushrooms, and the homemade whole grain toast. I ask for the soup and salad bar; I'm not very hungry. I wait until everyone's food comes before I go up to the bar. By the time I'm back at the table, Henry's food is almost gone. We sit at a square table: Henry across from me, his dad to my right, mom to my left. His dad likes to have us on either side of him because he's hard of hearing.

We talk about the dogs: mostly Happy's weirdness. Bird: how she escapes. How Raven seems to have gotten better—no recent attacks. Everyone loves Pip. When we visit Henry's parents' lake house Pip stays close to Bill. It's sweet to see a dog so small and fluffy and big-eyed with a man like Bill: tall and blind in one eye, with rough-looking skin, and he sort of hunches. Marylou looks great for eighty-one. She was a cheerleader for Texas Tech and can still fit into her uniform.

I mention to them again that tomorrow my son is moving. The movers came a week ago. My son and his wife are getting on a plane with their dogs and cat.

Henry and I hug his parents goodbye and thank them. Tell them that we love them. There's a fog in the air, and the slush from the road makes the ride home a little slippery. Henry is driving his Jeep with oversized tires. We ride down Center Road: a long path on the top of a hill that looks out to the ski slope.

Henry plays his surfing CD, which reminds me of our trip to Hawaii last year, him and his surfing lessons. He and my son out there in the ocean, and me, on the shore, with my daughter-in-law, collecting shells.

As Henry drives the fog thickens, it starts snowing again, and we're in a whiteout.

I say, It's like another planet.

As we get closer to home, things start to clear. Kissing Bridge, the slope, is packed. Figures skiing look to me like cursive. I say to Henry, It doesn't look like anyone is falling.

He said, Everyone is upright!

I take special notice of the magic carpet. I say, It's so packed. I'd knock over all the children.

When we're back home, Henry naps with the TV on to the Pro Bowl while I fidget with projects. Henry snores.

An enormous chunk of ice slides from the roof, bringing the new snow with it. It's like an avalanche. It makes a loud boom.

SNOW ANGEL

You're so pretty, I say to the sky. I get out my phone. I even take a picture.

I'm out on the skis I rented. It's my first time on these trails on skis, but not my first time out here. I've been on many trails here; my first time seeing Henry in person was on these trails. We'd been emailing. He was volunteering and I was running a race. At one of the stations, he handed me a cup of water. I waited for him after that. I journaled in my car. He didn't come out. I drove the hour home and didn't hear from him for a few days, and then he emailed, saying he'd been busy landscaping with his friend. Henry was mostly unemployed then.

This park is behind our house now.

I'm at the warming shack. It's where I met Henry for a run after we reunited. It was probably late spring. We ran up and down and around. After the run, we kissed. I felt young again, and sexy. We were sweaty and hot. I realized, after those four years, there was something about him I had missed. We kissed for a long time, and I said to him, Please, don't ever leave me.

I'm looking up now. The skis on my feet feel like long extensions of myself that don't really belong to me. I'd rather be on snowshoes. I try to think of all kinds of words describing how they feel: unconstitutional, misdemeanor, wombat, kitten. And then I figure I've been watching too much CNN and playing too much Wordscape.

I fall. I take off my skis and make a snow angel. The branches are still. The trees are filled with white. The sky is blue. I watch the clouds move.

HOLY COW

I get a ten-page letter from a prisoner in Alaska. Look at that flower, it starts. Written in pencil in all caps. I'm not sure how the prisoner got my address. It was sent to my office on campus. He says he's read my work. Mostly he talks about how the system failed him. His name is Bjork. He claims to be Norwegian. I'm Norwegian myself. The letter makes no sense, rambling about Cheez-Its. I used to get crazy letters from my father. Once he sent a Band-Aid, a note saying only Holy Cow, and a check for a dollar sixty-nine.

I go to the park, where I don my rental skis. I look up at the sky, seeing a jet far off: the trail it leaves. I wonder who's in the plane, imagine being up there. The world feels so quiet, like peace on a big speaker.

I move my arms, making my feet slide.

THE WHOLE SYSTEM OF THEM

These tomatoes even taste good, I say to Ben, the man I'm having lunch with.

He's in his seventies and serves on a board for my college.

He gets a Cobb salad, and I order the garden one with tofu.

His friend Walt is a friend of mine. Walt and Ben went to high school together. Last year Walt retired. He was an administrator at the college. Walt reads my books. He gave one to Ben and then Ben came to the restaurant on campus and Walt introduced us.

We're at the Saturn Club, an exclusive institution founded in the late 1800s, then for men. There's a gym and a pool. Marble floors. Lots of statues. A bar. There aren't any signs in front. It's big and brick, eccentric. High ceilings and stairwells shaped like rainbows. Everything is gothic-looking, with pictures of past deans on the walls. Some big architect designed the place. It's easy to get lost here.

Ben and I are in the Red Room. He's wearing corduroys and a matching mustard blazer and a bow tie. I'm wearing pants and a long sweater. Dansko shoes. There's a dress code. Blue jeans aren't allowed here.

I dip my lettuce into my balsamic. He forks his piece of shrimp and says, I'm not sure what Walt told you.

Walt told me some things. After one of the times Henry kicked me out of the house, Walt asked, What will you do? He'd asked, Are you in trouble? He made me promise I was fine. He says my work intimidates him. I remind him I write fiction.

I say to Ben, He told me the two of you are friends.

Ben says, How much do you know about campus politics?

I say, More than I should?

He sips through a straw.

The waiter wears a suit and tie. He asks Ben if everything's OK here.

The tables are set with white cloths, silverware and crystal, folded red napkins.

The fireplace is going.

Everything's fine, says Ben.

Ben talks about his kids. A daughter: an actress and model. His son is my age. I wonder if I know him. I talk about my son. I say, He's in the army.

Ben shows me a picture of his Poodle.

I show Ben pictures of Happy and Pip.

I say, Henry loves Trump and that's a problem.

Ben says, My son has properties. We can help.

ROOST

I meet my friend Gin at The Roost, a kind of hip spot not far from campus with big windows, lots of light, tall tables and chairs with narrow metal legs.

When I find her sitting by the window she gets up and hugs me. She has long brown hair, long legs and great posture. She's a runner, like me, was an English major in college and now works as an immigration attorney. She's a partner at her firm. She's here on her lunch break. It's Friday—I'm done with my first week back teaching and have just come from my office.

Whew! I say and sit across from her.

She says, Whew.

Her divorce is finally final.

I say, Lunch is on me today.

When the waiter comes, he recites the specials, lets us taste the wine. She orders Merlot and I get a sparkling white. We split a garden salad. I order lentil soup and she gets salmon.

She gives me updates—her girls are into gummy worms, one hating boys and germs. She has to pay alimony and child support. I talk about my son, who is in Tennessee now.

She asks, How're things with Henry?

I say, Same.

She's known us from our first time together, through the break-up and back. Henry knows her husband. We're all runners.

She'd invited me over to her place for Christmas after the last time Henry kicked me out. But then he invited me back and I figured I should save face and show up with him on Christmas at his parents'.

I'm sorry about Christmas, I say.

She says, Please.

I say, It's the politics. I think he's anti-women. He loves Trump. I just don't bring shit up anymore. I'm supposed to ski. I'm trying to ski. What's wrong with me?

She says, Nothing. You're amazing.

CRUISE CONTROL

I put on headphones, try to write on my computer, and imagine myself running, my feet on cruise control, my soul immune. With a set of prompt words, I go into a dream state. Today it's Yahtzee with my grandma. My mom saying to me: I'll be right back, and that seeming like centuries. Cooking for church bake sales. Root beer floats at A&W with my grandpa. Floats and pies and churches. Prayers and even more church and a lot more hands. Woods and pools and snow. How my paternal grandpa takes me for cruises on his snowmobile in the woods. Over the wide lake. How his fingers float. What is it about root beer? Beer? Roots? Boots and rear, and here I am again, instead of writing, finding myself playing word games.

I suggest skiing to Henry. I figure I should make an effort.

We go up the magic carpet. Henry swears there's something different about it.

I wear rented downhill skis. Before, I wore his mom's old ones. My last instructor said I should probably try some that weren't made before I was.

Henry bought himself a new jacket. He's wearing expert ski pants. His new helmet. He bought new skis for himself too.

When we reach the top, I hesitate. I stay for a while. The music that I hear from on the bottom is slight, with just a small hint of boom.

POLES IN THE GROUND

On the top of the slope, I imagine my son on his skateboard. He also snowboarded. In high school, buses would go out, full of kids, to the slopes. Now buses of kids come here. I see them when I drive by, and picture truckloads of small legs from all, with so much confidence under them. I remember kids from my own high school coming to class with ski passes hanging from their jackets. One of those kids, Marnie, took me out on her snowmobile once. She sped and said fuck a lot. I pretended to like it and held onto her jacket.

Growing up, I'd wake in the early morning, and run across the field to feed calves and milk cows. According to my mom, before our land was a farm, it was a swamp. In wet seasons, tractors sunk into the ground. In the winter, our garden turned into a skating area for my sister and me. My first time skating, my sister fell and broke her leg. I ran across the yard in my ice skates to get to the house to tell my mom we needed to get to the hospital.

Henry stands nearby, his poles in the ground.

I turn slow. Henry can ski backwards. Front and sideways. There aren't many other people here, save a couple kids who ski around us.

Henry says, Relax. Just follow.

I do that. I continue to go up the slope and down it. I hang on to him.

He says, Trust me!

I do it over and over, and I start to gain confidence.

MAGIC CARPET

Henry's new jacket compliments his eyes. He has nice eyes. Deep and green. They get red when he's tired. He has a nice nose, which he tells me he's conscious of, since it got broken. He has a plate in one of his cheekbones as a result of a fight when he was younger.

It feels kind of magical. I see the road across the highway leading up into our neighborhood.

As we ride up, Henry says that the last time he skied, he was mistaken for someone on ski patrol. He says, I was on the lift, and someone tried to convince me to work here.

I say, Do you want to?

He says, I'd have to re-certify. I'd have to take CPR classes on the days I'm not working.

I say, It's a good skill.

After we get to the top, he says, I saved a life once.

I say, I remember.

He retells the story of him in a car accident, and a woman had passed out. She didn't have a pulse. He remembered his training and simply lifted her chin. Put his finger in her mouth and dug her tongue out. He says, Then she started breathing.

That's good of you. You seem good at saving lives here.

He says, That's so sweet. You'll have to add it to my morning oatmeal.

I use my poles to push myself forward. I move my body like I'm dancing, as if the skis are a part of me.

I LET MYSELF GO

At the top again, I say to Henry, This is fun!

He stays put, watching me go downward.

I let myself go fast. I go up and down. It's Groundhog Day. I listen to the jibber-jabber on the speaker.

Later, at home, while he walks the dogs, I cook dinner: quinoa, salad. We watch the Super Bowl. He's for the 49ers. I'm take-or-leave: the Chiefs. We like the Bills. And also the Packers. I make popcorn and we talk about Pip's upcoming surgery, the dental work that'll cost me about a thousand dollars.

Poor Baby, he says.

Poor Baby, I say.

The dogs crowd around us.

The Chiefs win. In bed, Henry thanks me for a great day. He thanks me for a nice dinner. He thanks me for skiing with him.

We kiss a lot. He hugs me.

The next morning, I add extra berries to his oatmeal. I pack his lunch. He calls me around nine and says he has some news. He says, Which do you want first? The good news or the bad one?

THE ART OF FICTION

Henry says, I'm fired.

It's supposed to be his good news. When I ask him for the bad news, he says, I'm fired.

I say, I thought things were going good there?

He says, The bosses have been asses. I can collect unemployment.

I've been employed since I was fifteen. I've been working my whole life.

I say, What will you do?

He says, Probably get a haircut.

On my way to campus, I see his Jeep parked at the ski shop. A mannequin sits in the window. I have a little time, so I stop to say hi. Hi, I say to the mannequin. When I find Henry, he's near the back, talking to the woman who had helped me. I stand behind him and when he turns around, he jumps. He says, I was just talking about you.

The lady talks about downhill skis and I tell her the shorter ones suit me much better. She says I can keep them for the season and put that toward a purchase.

Henry says, I was just talking about you. I hope I didn't say anything bad.

His hair is trim. He kisses me, and, after we're outside, he talks more about how his bosses hate him. I tell him if there's anything bad he has to say about me, we can talk about that later.

He says, Stop.

It's about an hour drive to campus. I have classes. I talk to my students about the art of fiction.

TEETH

I take Pip to the vet.

The tech has forms for me to sign. The estimate. Henry had asked if I wanted him to take Pip. If he could help. I said, It's OK. If he wants, he can help after. The vet is about a twenty-minute drive and on my way to campus. I have a faculty meeting to attend, then a class to teach. Pip won't be done until after seven-thirty.

I do some work in my office—grateful for my private workspace. I have paintings on my wall: a collage my son made when he was in school: images of scissors, gum wrappers, a teardrop. I have a picture of him at four, in a Mickey Mouse hat. I have a picture of him in uniform. His graduation from army basic training. Another picture of him at the range with his rifle.

I read for the journal I edit. Stories and poems and nonfictions. I read a couple student stories: one from the point of view of a kneecap. When I go to the faculty meeting, our department chair holds up an ex-ray of his own knee. He's had a replacement.

I call the vet and the tech says Pip is doing fine. After classes, I call again and the tech says his teeth were worse than expected. They had to extract all but two. He won't be ready to be picked up for a while. I text that to Henry. He asks, Want to pick him up together? Grab a bite before?

We plan to meet at the Colden Country Inn at 6:30. It's down the road from where we live. Before I go there, since I have some time, I stop at the campus restaurant, where Kimmy pours me a glass of Prosecco and asks me how I am.

When I arrive at the Inn, I find Henry pulling up. We go to the back of the place where it's quiet. He orders a burger. I order a salad. He asks if I've been drinking. I say, I stayed on campus and had a glass or two with colleagues.

He says to me, Fuck you.

He gets up and leaves me at the table.

RAGDOLL

Pip's underbite no longer looks like an underbite with most of his teeth gone. The technicians have instructions: drugs every few hours. He's like a ragdoll. When I get home, Henry's on the sofa, TV on. My sofa. My TV. I pay the cable. His Internet. His phone. He's watching the Iowa caucus.

I have a flashback of him leaving me sitting there at the restaurant. I guess he had to go, I said to the waitress. ate my salad. I watched people at the other tables.

I'm trying to give Pip his meds. He's not opening his mouth. Henry's next to me, and I say, Can you at least help?

He says to me, Fuck you.

He calls me a cunt.

He says it over and over.

LATE NIGHT, GREAT NIGHT

I'm at Kissing Bridge and it's Late Night, Great Night. Because of snowfall, lots of places are closed: schools, church events, bingo. The Fish Fry at the VFW.

After Henry's verbal assault, I took Pip down to the guestroom, lay him next to me on the daybed. That's where I've been sleeping. Henry called me unreliable. Unreliable? I said. Who's the one without a job now?

That set him off. He said he wasn't sorry for calling me the c word. He said it over and over.

I even googled the word. It's the highest form of verbal assault on a woman there is. I texted Henry and sent him the link, and then the next day while teaching classes, I took about five different breaks so I could collect myself in the bathroom.

He told me to get out. I've started packing again. I took my art off the walls.

I said to him: You know we're just reacting. This isn't who we are. Will you go to counseling?

I'm sitting at the restaurant at the ski slope. It's busy and loud. I order French fries.

After Henry left the house, I came here to the ski place. I go up the magic carpet. I ski by myself. I know how to turn, stop, how to use the poles and when I get to the bottom, I go up again.

MY GOODS

After skiing, I go home to find Henry on the sofa. I see the back of his head, looking into his phone, a service I'm still paying for. The coffee table where he puts his feet is mine. The TV, too. Our bed.

Raven has even snipped at me a few times on that bed. I still have a scar on my hand.

He goes out to plow the driveway. I'm grateful for that. How else can I leave?

GUESTROOM

Wash your hair, I tell myself, looking in the mirror. Brush your teeth. Trim your brows. Hop in the shower. Shave.

Try to eat.

Henry's out skiing. When I woke this morning in the guestroom, I saw that he changed his status on Facebook to single.

I lay on the guestroom bed for a while. Bird comes down and hops in with me. Pip comes down too. I'm like a sandwich between them.

After a while, I go upstairs and start taking Henry's things off my table and put them on his loveseat.

My former neighbors have a guestroom. They've welcomed me to stay. It's right next to the house I had built, the one I sold before moving in with Henry.

BE NICE

From the guestroom at my former neighbors' house, I can see my former back yard. It's full of snow; I know under it is the vegetable garden I planted. Next to it is the baby peach tree that harvested peaches the first year.

I have nightmares of my father coming back to me under disguise trying to rape me. I have dreams about dreaming, about trying to feel and then not feeling and then waking into going back into my dreams and trying to recount them. I spend hours awake, flat on my back, hearing the hum of the traffic and a huge roar I can't source. It's like going back into a time zone.

I love this neighborhood, and I loved my house. After my aunt died, my uncle helped me pay for that house. I had to say and do things, be nice. I was vulnerable. I was grieving my aunt.

Things look a lot different from this side of the wall, this side of the window.

This development, even now, is new. This house, in Phase One, was the show house.

I talk to my depression. I get one leg out of the bed and then the other. I put myself into my car. I go to campus to teach and then I drive back to Henry's.

TRUST YOUR INSTINCTS

Henry's late to see the counselor. I made the appointment because he told me he'd left me alone at the restaurant for fear he was going to punch me.

I offered to pay for the session. I know we're over, but I have to protect myself. I need certain things in writing. I need to get out of his house, and I need to get out safely.

This morning in the nice clean kitchen of my former neighbors, I finally ate some toast. They left bread and peanut butter on the counter and a note that read, Help yourself. We're out at appointments.

After I fill out my paperwork, the therapist calls my name. Hers is Petunia. She asks me to explain the part about my partner maybe hurting me.

I say. I'm OK.

I've been watching too much *Dateline*.

I've been having dreams and flashbacks of those days with my ex-husband. Baby in my arms. When I ran, the husband followed. Barefoot, in Biloxi.

I talked to my son last night.

He said, Don't ever go back.

This appointment here? I'm surprisingly calm. I feel like I'm the smart one.

READING GLASSES

Henry texts. He's late.

I've started on his paperwork. Filling out what I can.

After he arrives, he apologizes for being late. He was out riding his bike. He forgot his reading glasses. I read him the questions.

LAND ON YOUR FEET

My aunt had a thing for butterflies. After she died, my uncle found a gold butterfly charm on a gold chain around her neck. He figured she bought it for herself. He bought her a lot of jewelry. They dated in high school. Prom queen and king. My uncle was Most Likely to Succeed. They went to school with my parents. My aunt was a beautician before working for my uncle's business.

My uncle gifted me that necklace. According to him and according to my aunt's best friend, I saved my aunt's life for a few months before she decided to take it. She'd gotten to a very bad place, not just with her cancer. She started to drink a lot. I asked her what she wanted. She didn't want to die. Pain was her worst fear. I'd give her whatever she wanted. She didn't want to drink. She quit, then went back to chemo. She started feeling better. I had to leave her in Wisconsin and go back to New York to teach.

Six months after I left, she was dead; my uncle confessed to me, that, since she had relapsed, he was about to kill her, then shoot himself to put them out of their misery. They were married over fifty years, and I was a baby at their wedding. He didn't want to kill her because she had cancer, he wanted to kill her because she drank too much. She had a complex relationship with my dad. He was her older brother. She didn't know what to do about his illness. The abuse my grandfather put onto them. He molested her. I questioned my grandfather's motives with me, after I grew into an adult. If we question things, there's a reason for the question.

TAX SEASON

When my house was being built, my uncle said we could pay cash for it. Encouraged every upgrade. But then he said: maybe you should get a mortgage? We can build your credit.

After my aunt died, and I was at their house, I had drinks with my uncle. I'd been spending a lot of time on my aunt's chair, the one she died on. With her blanket. I was wearing her clothes. My uncle told me I looked a lot like my aunt when she was younger.

The morning of her death, he left for work, leaving her in the recliner. It was tax season and they were accountants. After his day at work, he came home, and my aunt was in that same chair, same position. He asked if she wanted something to eat. Figured she was sleeping. He fixed himself some dinner, warming up chicken in the microwave. Turned on the TV. After a while, he got up to put his dishes in the sink. Then, on his way back to his chair, he touched her hand. It was cold. She was sitting upright with her head down.

My uncle slept with me. He took me to the bedroom. Where my aunt slept with him for years.

Was I complicit.

GETTING OUT OF IT

They say the best way to get through a captive situation is to build your captive's ego. You say things and do things: whatever it takes to make your captive feel in control. Your hope is to get out safely.

THE KEYS IN HIS POCKET

I'm back to get my stuff. Henry's cooked chicken on the grill. Eating it, along with the quinoa from the cabinet. He cuts his meat with my knife.

He says, I can't find my keys.

I go downstairs and find his ski pants. The keys are in his pocket.

SEEING PEOPLE RUN

Gin and I are at The Roost again. I'm wearing snow boots, a sweatshirt and black pants. She's wearing jeans and a running jersey.

She's helping me move what we can in my Mercedes and her SUV. I can't move into the new place yet, but Ben's son—my new landlord—is letting me put stuff in the basement.

Gin and I have the same waiter as last time: a young man in tight pants, red hair and a moustache. We order the salad we got the last time and cauliflower soup. We each order a Prosecco and once it comes, we toast.

Cheers! she says.

It's the day after Valentine's Day. Our glasses clink, we drink.

We eat our food. She talks about her newly-divorced life.

We've already taken one trip to Henry's and unloaded the stuff in my new basement.

We're about to take another.

She says, I'll be sure to watch the door.

At Henry's, Bird ran out while we were loading up our cars. We put Raven in the crate. Henry wasn't happy. Pip and Happy barked from behind the door in the guestroom. I text Henry and say we'll be back after lunch.

CHECK MY REFLEXES

My doctor asks if I feel OK. It's a physical. I tell him I feel fine.

He's thin. A runner. Kind. Soft-spoken. When I tell him I'm about to travel, he asks me: where to? There's a coronavirus going on.

My bloodwork is fine. There's nothing wrong with me. At my recent colonoscopy, a polyp was removed. He says it was precancerous. I say, It's good I had it done then?

He asks, Are you eating OK? Sleeping?

I say, Everything is fine. I'm a little stressed but am better since I'm moved now. A little syncope.

He listens to my heart. Looks into my mouth, asks me to stick my tongue out.

CAR WASH

I take my Mercedes to the car wash. Since the move, my car has gotten filthy. But I'm done now. Got everything out of storage. Movers have come for the big stuff.

My new place is a mile from campus—I still teach my classes. My art hangs on the walls. There's a hum of traffic. There's no loud shouting. No blaring TV. No Fox News. My dogs hardly even bark here.

Happy and Pip spend the day at the salon, getting their hair washed, cut and nails clipped, and leave with bandanas.

My new neighborhood is gritty with historic buildings, two blocks from the marina: the lake is so close! Across the lake I see Canada.

VIRUS

I fly to NYC for an awards ceremony hosted by Seth Myers. He laughs and says we're all sitting too close. Then I fly to Texas for a conference—lots of people opt not to come for fear of the virus.

I'm set in my apartment. Henry's agreed to keep my dogs for the week.

At the ceremony some of us do fist bumps, sneak hugs. We watch the news and wash our hands a lot.

It's a long flight home. The drive from the airport isn't as long as it used to be when I lived with Henry.

I take my bags up to the second floor. It's clean. Colorful. Artistic.

In the morning, I call Henry. When I get there, my dogs lick my face.

Happy's covered with scrapes and scabs.

Henry says, It's my fault. I left Raven's food out. Happy got to it and Raven wasn't happy.

I drive fast the whole way home.

TOUR GUIDES

All my classes are remote now.

In San Antonio, the day after the conference, I walked alone along the Riverwalk. Families and friends were out together, dining, shopping, laughing. I found a table at a restaurant, where I dined alone. I ordered greens. I got out my computer, responding to emails; I recalled my first visit to the Riverwalk—eighteen, my last weekend of air force basic training. Also, the same city where I later did my medical training, where I met the man who'd be my husband.

I walked. The conference was over.

I imagine lights and people on boats. Tour guides. Laughter. Ice cream.

In my new neighborhood, I take my dogs for a walk.

The virus has spread. The whole country, practically the whole world, is on some kind of lockdown.

MY SKIN IS SO MUCH SOFTER

My sister calls to say my uncle's dead. Probably his stent failed.

I was the one taking care of him and my aunt when the stent was placed all those years ago.

I have necklaces in my box, circles of infinities, gifts from him. I haven't spoken to him since I moved in with Henry.

My tub has claws. I pour a lot of water into it. I add salts. I soak myself clean.

RING ROAD

At Delaware Park, Ring Road, it rains and the trees look like origami. It's a familiar loop, one I used to run when I first moved to the city almost twelve years ago, where I'd go on training runs with a guy who tried to coach me. He said I was dynamite on certain runs, and sometimes in the bedroom.

On my first few dates with Henry we'd run here and I'd hear him breathe. We always seemed in step then, though I had to work hard to keep up, and we'd go out for a bite somewhere after.

The park is pretty bare now. I miss the bustle of bikers, children, people on the golf course. There's a zoo on one portion of the park and I see some cars there. The zoo is closed.

I breathe and take my steps.

I opt for another loop. My legs feel heavy. My heart feels heavy. My lungs are pretty healthy.

I extend my arms and pretend I'm flying.

BIRD ISLAND

Walking Pip and Happy on the Bird Island Pier, I see the highway, traffic, where I used to drive, on those long commutes, when I lived with Henry. I'd look along the water, wondering how to get to this strip of the walkway.

It's so close to where I live now.

I've swum in this lake with my triathlon club. I still fear the open lake, like it will swallow me like it swallowed my cousin's cancer. She died a year ago, and my first time swimming in Lake Michigan was with her, in our pre-teen years, and the undercurrent almost got us.

I read neighborhood signs that tell me of the Underground Railroad.

The pier is a long walkway. Birds sing and dance, the water does its surge, only miles on its way to Niagara Falls. My dogs seem happy. They stop to lift their legs and smell stuff. The sky is grey. Up above me is the Peace Bridge and across the water I see Canada.

I stop to read more signs that talk about the history. War. Now this whole world seems at war with a pandemic. I'm glad I'm not with Henry—we'd be arguing about his Trump views. I'd be working hard to defend my rights to be a liberal.

I feel odd and quiet, viewing one country and being in another, water's force between us. Hearing the whir and hum of the highway.

I keep going on the walkway and at its highest point, I stop.

The water moves. I am still, letting it move with me.

OCEANS AND PARKS

It's been fifty-one days since the fight with Henry.

My dogs look at me with heads tilted.

We can go to the movies, honey, I say to them. But we really can't. Everyone's on lockdown; I still take them to the parks. There are oceans of them! Ones Olmstead had created.

The dogs' limbs look tired. Their eyes are like questions.

TWO OR THREE TIMES

I meet my former neighbor Fay at Delaware Park, by the zoo. Buffalo eat hay and lounge behind bars.

When Fay and I were neighbors, we'd meet outside and walk the mile here, then circle Ring Road once, and sometimes two or three times.

My current apartment is a couple miles from here, in another direction.

We don't hug today, because of the virus.

She asks, How're you faring?

We walk briskly, at a steady pace.

Glad to be in the city again, I say. Thanks again for letting me stay at your place.

Anytime, she says.

So glad I got moved out before COVID.

THE HOSE AND THE REEL

I drive back to Henry's. I forgot my garden hose and reel cart. Henry used that hose to clean off his dirty bikes after his rides in the woods. It's just a garden hose. But it's the one I bought from Home Depot (along with the reel cart), after I had my house built. I had planted grass seed. I used it every morning, noon, and evening. I planted my own trees. I planted my own shrubs and flowers. My vegetables, my garden.

There's another hose of mine at Henry's but I told him he could keep it.

I texted Henry last night to ask if he would be there.

Henry said he hasn't been anywhere besides biking in the woods. He said he'd leave my stuff at the end of the driveway.

I bring Pip and Happy. I figure maybe I can take them for a hike in the woods.

When I get there, I fold down the back seats of my Mercedes. I lift the hose and reel cart. Henry comes out and asks if he can help.

He's in bike shorts and a short-sleeve shirt. His stubble is grey. He has to work a bit to fit the stuff in my car. I don't want to get too close, so I stand back.

We make small talk on his deck. He's still looking for a job.

I say, I'm taking the dogs for a hike.

He says, Want to bring Bird and Raven?

On the trail, the dogs' paws thump, and their nametags are like chimes. The sun is out, the trees are bare, save a few things budding. It smells like the spring it is! I retrace old steps, passing stumps and branches, crossing the creek I fell into on my bike when the creek seemed frozen.

AN ODE TO APEXES

My dogs let me sleep in every morning.

The mattress in the guestroom is comfy, and the frame is broken, so the mattress just sits on the floor. Some nights I write here. I watch CNN. Cuddle with Pip and Happy. Sometimes I fall asleep to the TV. Some nights I get up and go to the master bedroom, which is clean and organized. Most nights I fall asleep in one bed, wake in the night and move to the other.

These days I wake usually by eight, and when I start to move around, the dogs look at me. Happy finds a toy and chews on it and flops around. Pip's eyes get bright. I'll get up and make some toast, feed them. Happy's always done first. They're patient with each other. Sometimes Pip licks Happy: his ears, his legs, his paws.

Lately, at night, I watch the governor on TV, updates on the virus. Fauci. He works, to some extent, with my ex-husband.

Will a curve ever be the same? I imagine apexes all over the world, shifting and changing, rising and descending.

ZOOM

I hear the hum of the interstate, an army of thunder.

Since my classes have gone remote, I do discussion boards. I've taught online before, so the transition isn't hard. I attend video meetings with colleagues.

I talk to my uncle's sister. The attorney's offices are closed. Banks are doing minimal things. I wonder if she goes onto his computer.

There will be no memorial.

I take long baths. Soaking. Nurturing my skin with berry-smelling lotion.

PUMPKIN

At night, I dream of reaching out to someone. My dogs sit with me as we watch CNN. The *Tiger King*. The cats in the film remind me of Raven. Henry feeding her, the alpha, calling her his pumpkin.

NERVES

Once, years ago, during my first time with Henry, I woke with a numb hand. Couldn't move my fingers. Couldn't move my wrist. Couldn't open doors nor brush my teeth nor even eat right. It was my right hand and of course I'm right-handed. I called my doctor, who rushed me to the neurologist, who said she didn't think I had a stroke. I eventually had a nerve test, which indicated my nerve had been compressed. I've always been a hard sleeper. It took months to get my hand back.

Tonight on CNN the governor's brother talks about his COVID symptoms. Soldiers become celebrities, along with those in healthcare.

I know about masks, PPE, gamma globulin, antibody testing. I worked in a blood bank during Desert Storm, collecting and processing products. My husband at the time was sent to England to set up a contingency hospital similar to the ones I see on the TV at Central Park now. Our son was a baby.

My ex-husband, now with the NIH, texts me with his updates.

BUFFLEHEAD

As I notice birds in the yard, I include at least one bird as a prompt for the online writing group I've been hosting for almost twenty years. Today is Bufflehead. They are small ducks that "dive underwater to catch aquatic invertebrates. When courting females, male Buffleheads swim in front of them, rapidly bobbing their heads up and down. In flight, you can identify Buffleheads by noting their small size, fast wingbeats, and patterns of rocking side-to-side as they fly."

I take heed of the open call from our governor. New York: in need of qualified lab techs to do COVID testing.

Classes are still remote.

I update my resume. Recall my years in blood bank, hematology, microbiology, urinalysis, phlebotomy, parasitology, serology, chemistry. I'm still certified. I send in my applications. It's been fifteen years since I worked in the lab. The hospitals are desperate. How else can I help?

THIS PLACE WHERE I LIVE

On a dog walk, I see a man on the corner by the bus stop. Sprawled out on the lawn. I keep my distance. I hear the hum of the interstate, see the sunset as it falls onto the water. There are train tracks up ahead. Signs on lawns provide each building's history. 1823, 1838. When Black Rock was a hub. It's before the flu of 1918 that killed my maternal great-grandfather. My grandfather was only seven months, and his mother had six other children.

My great-grandmother remarried not long after, to a man with even more children. I remember family gatherings, full of cousins, aunts and greats. So many parties at the house where my grandmother was born. She also lived and died there.

That big house is gone now. The century farm. Same as the other century—the one where I grew up.

Upon returning home, I search my pockets for my keys. They're missing. I stand outside the door. I try to turn the knob.

My pockets are filled with poop bags. My phone.

I sit on the front step and text my landlord. He lives across the street in the renovated firehouse.

He texts and says, Didn't the last tenant leave you with her spare one?

No.

He says, Let me check. I'll call you.

It's dark, save the city lights.

After we hang up, I walk down the street again. The man on the corner is still there on the grass.

I approach him, giving him six feet. Are you OK? I say.

He grabs his knees. Nods. He mumbles something.

I say, Do you need help?

He says, Please leave or I'll hurt you.

DISNEYLAND

Henry has one last thing of mine. When I lived with him, I purchased masks and gloves for cleaning.

Everyone needs masks now. I never thought I'd need them, at least not for a mandate. Now there's a shortage, and people are making masks of their own.

Passing the slopes, thick stripes of snow still make themselves apparent. The place usually stays open into April, full of bands and concerts.

At the door, his dogs jump. They bark. He puts leashes on them and comes out with the masks.

We keep our six-foot distance.

I have my dogs too. They're leashed.

He hands me the masks.

I say, Maybe keep one for yourself? He hangs one on the handlebar of his bike, which is propped next to his firewood.

We make small talk about his potential job at the post office. It's all fucked up, he says, and vents about working maybe at one place, then another. He breathes hard. He's wearing paint-splattered pants.

HOW DOES YOUR GARDEN GROW?

I take my dogs to my back yard. It's fenced. I free them of their leashes. They sniff and pee. There's still a nip in the air. The sun is out and flowers start to bud. Purple ones, some yellow. I don't know what they are but will look them up and figure. There's a pear tree that will produce lots of fruit come summer. Oh, summer, spring, I love you.

BORDER PATROL

My son was due to deploy to the Middle East today to fight off insurgents. But because of the virus, he was flown to a border in Texas. His job will be to alert Border Patrol if there's anything alarming.

I'm sitting on a chair, on the phone with him, and I say, Remember the siskins?

Mom, he says, I know.

The day we first moved into our home in England—he wasn't even two—a big flock of siskins landed on our lawn. My son pointed out the window. It was the first time he said: sing!

My dogs run around. Pip sprints in circles. Happy's finally lost the weight he gained from living with Henry.

I tell my son, I applied for lab jobs. I heard back from one today. I figure maybe I can help. Make some extra income.

He says, That's noble, Mom. Be safe.
I say to him, You too.

I'M STILL A LITTLE SASSY

Do our ancestors speak to us? I feel the vibrations of them humming on my eyelid. Taste them on my tongue. My maternal grandfather, who served in the second world war, used to single me out from the other grandkids, thank me for my service. If he were still alive, would he be proud of my son, who serves in the army? My grandmother used to tell my grandpa that it wasn't fair to the other grandkids that he spoke so highly of me, of my service during war.

Do you know what it means to be at war?

Maybe I'm still a little sassy. She used to call, told me to be careful. But I know that's just projection. Of course she was worried.

My grandfather died blind, but the last time I saw him, in assisted living, he knew who I was as soon as I walked into the room.

JUNCO

My shoulders are like yolks, my spine a shell. My body a ball of inflammation.

I've been eating healthy. Making juices in my juicer. Running, walking dogs. Logging everything in.

But my sciatica is back. Shooting pains down my leg.

Junco birds land on the tops of the fence in the yard. I sit here with the dogs because I can't bear to walk them.

The birds are like helium fur. Go naked, they say to me. I call them silly pupils. An eye to my temple, my forehead, the wearing-a-tie me, which I had to do in the video in last night's Zoom production—it's like a big word game.

I resort to my own tub. Fill it up.

I sink into the hottest water where I watch a video of Chris Cuomo talking about the best ways to kill a virus.

Fever dreams.

I sink and I soak and I sink and I soak, falling asleep, having dreams of my own.

BUTTERFLY WINGS

I'm on my back and trying to move my mind into my body, relaxing the parts of me that are contracted.

In my bedroom is a painting of a swallowtail. With a loon, a violin, a moon. Something I made in a college art class. Butterfly wings take up half the painting.

I send out more applications to the labs. Oh, the clicking of machines. The look of cells under the scope. The matching up of blood types.

A talent agent from a local hospital emails to ask about my license. I don't have my New York State one. In the works, I say. A recruiter calls to say he's gotten my profile in as well. Can you travel? Don't you want to work medical full-time? Your license doesn't matter. I can put you outside of New York! We can wait. We want you! And besides, I hear New York is speeding these along.

I teach. Answer students' questions. Read their work. I have a Zoom meeting with colleagues who are concerned about enrollments.

My dogs lay around, alternating between the floor, the beds, the sofas.

I wait for calls from hospitals. I text my son and ex-husband on a three-way message. I tell them about the steps of getting the New York license. Only one of three states for which it's required. My son asks: do you need help covering that? The expense, I mean?

I tell him that is sweet. I tell him I am fine now.

I HAVE SOMETHING FOR YOU

I get a call from some financial place. There's an IRA. An inheritance. This is not a scam. This is from my aunt. This is from my uncle.

THIS ENORMOUS CURVE

Most of the guys on the dating site are in Toronto, and who knows when we'll cross the border? There's an actor, a producer. Guys, posing at angles. A local guy, a carpenter, sends me head shots, pictures of him cooking, using rosemary and lemon, pictures of his butter lamb. Another guy shows me the picture he captured of a sandpiper with its wings spread. Another guy's picture reveals a close-up of his teeth.

I'm not meeting anyone in person for a while yet.

I stay home.

On TV, the governor says the curve is starting to flatten.

I dance around my apartment with my dogs and celebrate the curves of my own.

ANTIBODIES

I empty the last boxes.

After I moved into my apartment, in one of my frenzies, I took trips to Walmart, Target, bought myself new bookshelves, which I put together, following directions. The pandemic wasn't quite a pandemic yet.

There are four new bookcases in this last room. I sit on a pillow-like chair that used to be in my office on campus.

I try to find resumes of my days in the lab. I explain to potential employers why I haven't worked in labs for so long. I hear all the talk on the news about antibody testing.

I recall results, tests coming through. Positive, negative, inconclusive. Spectrometers and microscopes. A lot of these tests are run by big machines. You have to calibrate. And when the machines break, you have to do everything by hand. You have to know the theories.

I can look under that scope. Pipette. See colors, cells. Morphologies.

I find tax paperwork. Paperclips and envelops and stamps. A bullet from my maternal grandpa, saved from the second world war. Tokens and treasures. My desk is old and wide and deep. The desk itself was originally owned by a college professor from Hungary who isn't with us any longer, either.

After the last box is empty, I break it up, fold it, take it out for recycling.

I teach. I am eager for calls from the labs. From the state, regarding my license.

I move from cushion to cushion, to the next room full of cushions. I stretch out my back. I alter my body, ease into my mind. Remind myself to relax.

HEMOCHROMATOSIS

I hear the hum of the buses, the cars on the interstate, but they're so constant, like the fan I used to turn on when I was in college and working night shift. It helped me sleep. Sometimes, though, after a night shift, I'd start to fall asleep on the highway, so I'd pull in to a rest stop.

By the time I'd get home, I was awake again, and picking up my son to take him from one place to another.

I tried to balance between being a mom, working as a med tech and my college education, in my quest to be a writer.

I sign up for online classes called things like Ironing Out the Problems in Hemochromatosis, A Novel Pathogentic CALR Exon 9 Mutation in a Patient with Essential Thrombocythemia, A Reflex Protocol for Creatinine Testing Reduces Costs and Maintains Patient Safety.

I don't know what these things mean. I figure I can learn.

I look around my room. Colorful, so bright. I put my hand to my chest, feeling the heart of me.

IT REQUIRES A CERTAIN TOUCH

I used to be the kind of nerd who would read everything on health. The best way to eat, falling into all the trends: step classes and aerobics. In Biloxi, I became an instructor.

It was a side job. I was working in the lab then, poking infants' heels, a capillary test: I made sure to warm the heel first. I'd milk it, like I used to milk cows' teats on the farm in Wisconsin. I had to pipette.

I prepared my soundtrack. Janet Jackson's "Nasty," Paula Abdul's stuff, Madonna, and Milli Vanilli. I wasn't a good instructor. I tired everyone out and they left the class early.

I'm learning to relax. I research birds. I wonder if they have egos? In their wings, when they decide to lift them?

RULES OF ENGAGEMENT

What's the R.O.E.? I see in the group text my ex-husband sends to my son and me.

I text, What's an R.O.E.?

My ex, after our son's basic training graduation in Georgia three years ago, took a tour with his wife and our son and me of the infantry museum. There was a statue of a soldier's brain, and my ex said he held the real brain in his hands once.

R.O.E., I learn, means Rules of Engagement.

My son says, Site security only.

GIRL

During my first days working in the lab—after tech school, I was an intern. My then-future-now-ex-husband had been there months already. He was smart. He had a car.

We met in the hospital cafeteria. I was with my roommate who I went to basic training with, then tech school, and we both moved on to Lackland. She didn't take shit from anyone, said "girl" a lot. Approaching an empty booth with our trays, the two guys at the next booth came and sat with us.

Girl and me: we were the new ones.

I was 19.

My first days there involved phlebotomy. We had fears of AIDS. It was 1988. Patients would come with huge pink stickers on their binders. We could tell who they were before the binders came in. We wore gloves. Those patients required fifteen tubes.

I can still draw blood in my sleep. I still notice veins. Imagine a needle entering the best one, the blood shooting through the tube, then testing.

I miss seeing the data coming out of the machine.

I have a phone interview with a lab manager on Friday.

GO TO THE MALL

First I have a phone session with my guide where she takes me back to my past with my family. Pumpkin pies, with my mom and dad, my sister and my grandma. Jasmine rice with my ex-husband and his mom, who made black beans and lots of dishes from where she grew up in Jamaica. I've been cooking a lot, since we're all on lockdown.

It's April and the snow falls. Cars on Ring Road are no longer allowed (because of COVID), so I park on the street by the zoo. I take a chance on my back again. My dogs and I walk into the wind. We used to come here often, when I lived closer, after I had my house built. During that time, I also bought a lot of new outfits. Now they all sit in my closet. My accessories are glasses, a hat, a mask.

When I was a teen, after my mom left my dad and I moved with my mom and sister to Green Bay, after my new school, when I didn't have some kind of sporting practice, and when I wasn't serving ice cream at the job where I worked, I was by myself a lot. My sister fell into her studies and I fell into my shopping.

I figured out the buses. I got to know the schedule.

I'd go by myself to the mall. I'd buy the cutest outfits. I'd buy shoes, and shirts, and lipstick. Eyeliner. I'd stay until the mall closed with just enough money for the fare to get home.

TICK TOCK

I stay up too late. I've discovered TikTok.

There are dogs and babies and couples jumping on each other. A foot game, recipes, a partridge in a pear tree.

There are hospital workers dancing in their scrubs with masks and gloves, the videos only lasting seconds.

I review lab terms. Wonder where my scrubs are. There's an ASCP Virtual Town Hall on Monday. American Society for Clinical Pathology. Calling on the government for help. National COVID-19 Diagnostic Testing and Support Strategy. I can Zoom in and hear from the experts.

Microbiology, serology, immunology, parasitology, urinalysis, hematology and blood bank. Phlebotomy, virology, histology, cytology. Coagulation. Using microscopes. Pipettes!

I dress up, scarf and all. I put my phone on speaker. Interviewers ask me things like: what's your story?

I go through my past of working labs. Here and there and here and there and then here and there and then there and here again. I don't remember instrumentation as much as I remember the smell of plasma in the thawer. Specimens. Bleach. The powder from the latex. Petri dishes. No growth, some growth, the spread of E. coli, Pneumococci. Gram positive, gram negative. Streptococci. The shape of blood cells under scopes: reds, and whites (neutrophils, eosinophils, blasts), the clumping of small platelets, like huddles in a team.

What would make me a good member of *their* team?

I have lots of energy.

Where do you see yourself in five years?

Maybe I'll build another house. Maybe I'll get to see my friends. Maybe I'll get to see my mom, my son, my sister and her family. Maybe I'll travel to India, to Rome, to Hong Kong. To Antarctica, Australia. Maybe I'll swim again, one day the ocean. Maybe I'll take trips to the mall. To my stylist. Maybe I'll finally get my hair cut.

I don't say these things, of course. For now, I just say, Hmm. This is a really good question.

FOUND MATERIALS

The coffee percolates, and I put a vegan Just Egg on the pan, adding the herbs I bought from my last masked trip to the grocer. Sage and basil, dill and marjoram, cilantro. Chives. A few bits of an onion. Salt and pepper. I put two slices of Ezekial bread in the toaster, and I open the curtains.

One my favorite rituals: opening the curtains, signifying the start of a new day.

I feed my dogs. Scooping the food from the big bag in the corner. Happy inhales his food, then watches Pip as he finishes.

I find mustard from the fridge, a beefsteak tomato. I put the toast on a plate, add the mustard to each slice, cut a thick slice of the tomato, add it to the toast. I flip the food, add half a slice of vegan cheese on the top of it. Pour myself some coffee. Add a teaspoon of raw honey to the coffee, a good portion of soy milk.

The sun shines. The kitchen has two windows. The dining room has two. The dining room opens to the living room, where my plants big as trees absorb the light the bay windows invite in.

I turn off the burner, put my food on my toast. Take my plate and my coffee into the dining room. Set them on the table. I put the stuff on the counter away and wash my pan. I like to have the kitchen clean before I eat at mealtimes.

On the wall, here, from where I sit, I see the photo of the shearwater bird I'd taken when visiting my son in Hawaii. Its wings spread. On my desk sits a piece of coral I collected on a hike with him.

The dogs stay at my feet.

I eat my food. I sip my coffee.

I say to Pip and Happy, We'll go out soon.

I take another bite. My back is feeling better.

The day's only getting started. I feel safe here, in my home. I eat my meal.

I savor, sitting at my table.

SANTA IS A TEASE

Let's have a party, I say to the dogs. We're in my Mercedes, heading to the park.

I talk to my dogs, like the dolls of my childhood. I imagine putting the dolls in my car, making them do somersaults around me.

The dolls sit on a chair in my guestroom. One is toddler-sized: Chrissy, whose arms and legs move. She's blonde, but missing hair chunks. She wears pink pajamas—a one-piece with a zipper in the front and footies—I wore this as a toddler. In a picture of me, I'm wearing that outfit, and my sister's with me, wearing one that matches. Another doll is Baby Tenderlove, who I got for Christmas when I was maybe four. There's a picture of me opening her box, a gift under the tree. Baby Tenderlove's arms and legs don't move. She's always in the same position, her eyes fixed. I used to clothe her in a diaper, wrapping her in blankets. Carry her around. Rocking her. Saying, Shhh. It'll be OK now.

I had a Drowsy doll, gifted to me another Christmas; at first Santa passed out presents to everyone in the family except me, and said I wasn't getting one because I broke the cookie jar. I'd only wanted a cookie. I didn't mean to break the jar. Then, after I ran upstairs crying, my mom came up and said that Santa is a tease. I was five. I didn't know then that Santa was a relative in a suit. I got my gift and that was Drowsy. Years later, Drowsy disappeared, and when I asked my mom where Drowsy went, she said I had outgrown her.

At the park, my dogs sniff and lift their legs. The sun shines, people walk and run and bike and rollerblade. The golf course is closed. The zoo, too. People wear masks. The dogs pull on their leashes when they see other dogs. I wave to people far off.

I avoid the concrete path, prefer the grass and cinder. I stop to stretch, keeping my legs straight, hands on my lower back, leaning. My dogs stay with me. I tell them, Shhh. I say, Don't be a tease now.

CHICKADEE-DEE-DEE!

I plant Cucamelon seeds in small pots, leave them by the window that lets in the most sun. When it warms and the seeds begin to sprout, I'll put them in the yard. Along the edges of the fences are little gardens of weeds and plants; what they exactly are, I don't really know yet.

My landlord has people tend to the yard, and the neighbor downstairs says the yard is neat, come summer. I think of days ahead, sitting out there with my dogs, on the big, long table, maybe reading, writing. I'll pull the weeds, though I hope I don't pull anything that's fruitful.

A table by a window holds herbs. Basil, rosemary, thyme. I've put a bridle on my mint plants. I drop its leaves to my teapot, adding honey and ginger to my cup. It soothes my stomach, like seeing the chickadee feeding itself upside down. Chickadee is one of my prompt words for today. Do you know the chickadee can expand its hippocampus in spring by thirty percent so he/she can remember their cache sites—because they're hoarders? They look for things like trees to give them special clues. Oh, and their sound! Chickadee-dee-dee! If I put out my hand, will they come to me?

Cuca melons are termed as "little pops of acid." They look like tiny melons, taste like cucumbers. I bought some from the co-op before lockdown, and since then, have not been able to find them. I ordered seeds online.

These nights, I sleep well. I wake in the morning, open shades, and make myself breakfast. Walk the dogs. Maybe do a workout. Take a bath. Write and read and stretch. Call friends. Clean. Cook. Meditate. Take care of my plants. Take care of my body. I imagine gardens and gardens and gardens, like the home where I grew up, the farm where I grew up, where my parents grew up and their parents and their parents. All those farms are gone now or belong to other families. I'm in another state, but oh, who says I can't grow a farm of my own?

I CAN DO ANYTHING

I'm on a group call, hearing budget numbers. Recapping our last conference.

I get an email from the Human Resources person at the hospital system where I interviewed. She says they want to hire me but can't do so until I get my New York license.

I write. I walk the dogs. I clean. Clean, clean. Getting down to the corners. I put lemongrass oils in my aromatherapy diffuser. Talk with my financial advisor, who works with me through investments, my retirement, my future.

In the mirror, I find wrinkles on my skin. Focus on the scraggly ends of my hair, my dark roots growing, the blonde color getting brassy. I imagine a new look. I had no hair until I was four. My son shaves his head and I don't know how long it will be until I can see my stylist. Because of the pandemic, even she is closed now.

I imagine going to Brazil, hanging out with antwrens. Maybe building a new house again. Maybe flying everywhere, with the birds, all over the world.

I take the kitchen scissors to my hair. I cut and cut and cut.

Then I find the razor.

I figure my hair is beyond saving at this point, so I might as well shave it.

FOUR AND FIVE AND SIX

I send a picture of myself to my son, and he says, Why'd you do that?

I figure by the time my hair grows, maybe my stylist will be open. My son shaves his head because of his receding hairline. My aunt wore hats and wigs the last years of her life. My mom's hair is thinning. She lets it grow long, only to tuck it up, under hats, under the wigs she custom orders.

I send my stylist a picture of my shave and she asks my reasons. I remember the time she shaved her head. It grows back. You can color it and do all sorts of shit. I give her the same reasons I provided to my son. She says, Fuck yeah. You rock it. She says she misses hair. She needs to be around it.

I get another call about a lab job. From the cancer institute. Am I available for an interview?

I have a session with my guide on FaceTime. If we go on a journey, where to go?

After we switch from the video to phone and I lay flat on my bed, she guides me down one and two and three, four and five and six, seven and eight, and nine and ten, and I'm on a cloud. I picture myself floating on a field, in a minefield of flowers, feeling the colors of them. I stay there for a long time, and before we sink into another state, I go back to the hills of Austria, where I'm in the mountains, the place where I went with my aunt, on a physical vacation. It's where she had asked me to spread her ashes. She hasn't left. She asks me where I've been. She says she's been waiting.

PEDESTRIAN

On a path circling Hoyt Lake, I walk my dogs.

The water is calm. It's cloudy, cold. Yesterday was rainy. On a normal day, when there isn't a virus, folks might be out on canoes. This lake is across the street from one of the art museums. Steps from my campus office. I haven't been there lately.

My phone rings. It's my son.

Hi! I say. He takes me through my walk. I pass over the pedestrian bridge, over the 198, then to the other side of the park to Ring Road, where my son and I talk about money and investments. Education. My history and his. Exercise. His dogs and my dogs and his cats. He's still in El Paso.

We talk of the last election. Then he was in basic training. Since he didn't have access to the news, I mailed him clips every day. It was one thing he had asked for.

How did we last almost four years? I say. I stop to let the dogs pee.

It seems like ten.

I pass by the buffalo, other people on occasion, giving us our distance.

We talk about bare heads.

I smell the air. My dogs stay by my side.
It's a gift to feel alive here.

BUZZ CUT

I wake from another dream of being lost. I leave my bike somewhere but can't find it. The landscape has turned itself around. Everyone else seems to know where they are, watching a game, keeping score, and I'm on my own, sweating up a hill, daffodils waving.

It's a rainy morning—I open the curtains. The dogs beg at my feet. It's past nine a.m. I go to the front porch, collect the Sunday paper.

Throughout the day, the dream stays with me. It brings on memories of other dreams. Not able to find my car. Missing flights. Losing my phone. Losing my wallet. Losing my connections.

I look into the mirror, pluck my brows. I study my jawline. I run my hands over my head.

Everything is smooth now.

BE NICE TO THE ANIMALS

Be nice to the animals, I imagine my aunt saying, wherever she exists now.

After my maternal grandfather died, I had a trip planned to Key West with a boyfriend. I called to ask my aunt: should I go back to Wisconsin? Or should I vacation?

She said, You already said goodbye. I imagine heaven a place with all the animals. Dogs and cats. Maybe even turkeys.

I went to Key West. I paid tribute to my grandfather. He was a fisherman. That boyfriend chartered us a boat and we caught small fish, put them in a bucket that we'd later used for shark bait.

When the captain brought us to shallow water, we waited like statues. The expanse of the water was like a giant lawn.

Sharks started to swarm in.

I wore a harness. Once one shark neared, I baited it, hooked it. It took me a whole hour, using all my strength to get the shark close enough to the boat for a picture and let it loose again.

SQUARE

It's another day of Zoom meetings with my colleagues. I wear a cap.

My colleague John texts and says, I like your hat.

I look at his square on the screen, see him sip from his cup.

I say, I shaved my head.

He says, Send pictures!

I say, You got it.

He says, Once we're safe, I want to see your place.

I quit the dating site. I watch CNN—the virus is up and down, all over.

I WAS FIVE

I have a Zoom session with my guide and she takes me back to that Christmas when I believed in Santa. I return to the time when I was five and broke the cookie jar. Everyone laughed and I ran upstairs to the bedroom.

My guide takes me on a journey finding angels, my young self and myself-self. She takes me through a door, a cloud.

I lay comfy, in my bedroom.

She also brings me to my uncle. I got to love him deeply. He made me feel special. He was also my uncle.

I long for my old home. The one he helped me build. I grieve for him. I grieve for my childhood.

When my guide brings me back, I open my eyes and see a room full of color, lights, better things ahead.

HEAD SPINS

The syncope is back. I stand, hold onto the wall during the head spins. I remind myself to hydrate.

I take the dogs to the park. They wait in the car while I run a loop at Ring Road. The sun is out. The temp is in the 50s

I listen to Max Richter. The music lifts me. I take in the air.

I do a second loop. The park is empty.

I get to the car, remove my dogs, and take them with me on yet another loop, in a downpour.

ZIP ME UP

I'm on my knees, putting on my wetsuit.

I'm with athletes from my triathlon club, at Wilkeson Pointe: a spot off the lake.

The water is 62 degrees. I ask one of my teammates to zip me. I put on my swim cap.

I swing my feet on the dock, next to one of my team members in his late sixties. He says, Women first.

He points ahead. Swim there, he says, across then down again. He says he will swim with me. I haven't swum outside in years, since I lived with Henry.

I dive in. Feeling the water on my face, my hands, my feet.

I move my arms, my legs, rotating my whole body, kicking and extending.

HOW TO FIX A FLAT

At the bike shop, I walk in with my helmet on—some things are open again, though we still have to mask.

Henry works here now. He knows I planned to come. I'm here to buy another road bike. I've been riding a lot lately. My other road bike's old.

He looks nice. He's wearing the casual cycling jersey that I bought him. He's wearing casual pants. He looks as if he's had a recent haircut.

I say, Hello.

Oh! he says, Hello!

While he helps another customer, I browse the accessory section: bike tools, clothes. Other bikes and still even more bikes.

Cycling shoes. I talk with some of the other customers: all of us distant with our masks on.

When Henry finally finds me, he points and says, You're next.

His mask is a light blue, with a collage of dogs on it. He has light-colored eyebrows that arch just above the tip of the darkest parts of his eyes.

I say, I like your mask.

He leads me to the front.

All the stores are low on bikes now.

The bike is white. It looks a little small. Very light. Also very fancy. It's a Fuji. It's priced at over five-thousand. It's a 2012. Marked down to just over a thousand.

I say, That's a nice price. Do you think maybe it's too small, though?

He says, You're wearing your helmet. You can take it for a test ride.

He puts pedals on it, raises the seat. I watch his hands.

He says, How're the boys?

I say, Happy's lost weight. Pip sprained his shoulder. I bought him a stroller. I've been walking them a lot.

I say, How are yours?

He tightens things.

He says, They don't like it that I'm working. Bird ran off again. Took me hours to find her.

He points to the battery, the gears. He says, The gears are electric. Take it out. See how it goes.

I mount the bike. I point to the right and say, That way?

He points the other way and says, That way's a dead end.

I say, How long do I have? What time are you done here?

It's 4:30.

He works until six. The store closes at eight.

I ride to the dead end. The seat's too low. I feel as if I'm riding a kid's bike.

When I get back, he's waiting.

As he raises the seat, I say, How long have you been here?

He says, About three weeks.

Liking it?

We've been busy.

I want him to take his time. I want him to hurry up. I want to stay here and watch him. I want to run away.

I take the bike out again to the dead end. The seat's still too low and I can't seem to shift the gears right.

When I get back, he's waiting. I say, The seat needs to go higher.

He adjusts the seat more. He says, I have some of your things in my Jeep. Some clothes. Shoes.

I say, I've been missing a couple shoes. I wondered where their strays went.

I ride the bike down the dead end again. It feels better. It's a nice bike. It's growing on me.

But I still can't shift the gears.

He's waiting for me again.

I say, I don't think the gears work.

We bring the bike to Greg, the mechanic. I've known Greg as long as Henry.

While they figure out the battery, I look around the store some more. Accessories. I say to a guy with toilet paper taped to his nose, I like your mask.

Henry brings the Fuji out to me and says, There was a spare battery in the back. I raised the seat some more.

I take the bike down the busy street, hearing the loud traffic, feeling the whoosh of cars and trucks as they pass. The bike feels good. Do I want it? Do I need it? Do I want it? Do I want it? Do I want?

When I get back to the shop, I say, I want it.

When he sold cars, he sold me my Mercedes.

After the bike is ready, Henry throws some water bottles in the mix. The store only has Christmas ones left. The colors match my bike, and Henry says, Your bike looks like Christmas.

I present my credit card and pay.

He walks me to my Mercedes. I pop the trunk. The bike won't fit, so he removes a tire.

We walk to his Jeep. I say, Have you been out with the doors off?

He says, Not yet. It takes a lot of work, with the hard top.

He gives me the bag of my stuff. I didn't realize I left so much.

He says, There's probably more.

As we walk back toward the shop again, I say, Thanks for the bargain.

He says, I hope it works for you.

He looks at his watch.

It's six p.m.

I say, Time to go?

He says, I have to wrap things up here.

I stop at the park on the way home. I take the bike out of the trunk and I put it back together. I ride laps around Ring Road, speeding on the downhill.

TIME TRIAL

Tonight's my triathlon club's time trials in Grand Island.

I pop my trunk, remove my bike.

My friend Kit is here, putting her shoes on.

I met her running. She's in my age group. Faster.

I show her my new bike. I say, I bought it from Henry.

She says, Ah! Like your Mercedes.

This time's a little different.

She inspects the bike and says it looks fine. She inspects my biking shorts and asks me where I got them.

Amazon, I say. Thirty bucks. They have a lot of cushion.

She says, So are you done with classes?

Just put grades in.

I love your hair!

It's growing out some. I finally saw my stylist. She colored it platinum.

I say, Have you heard from Gin?

Not lately. How's she been?

We talk about tonight's route. About the races that are canceled. The pandemic. Weather.

We go out on our ride. She goes first. This is not a group ride. We try to ride our fastest. Eighteen miles. This path is different than the one I used to ride—I haven't been active in the club since Henry. This route is on a bike path. This one has no potholes. I feel like I'm flying.

HIDE UNDER THE BED

At home tonight, it's hot, and since there's no AC, I leave the windows open. Fireworks go off. It's not even July yet. All over there've been riots.

My poor dogs whimper, hide under the beds.

TAKE ME HOME

Today I ride the hybrid—I'd bought it so I could ride with Pip: I have a seat for him, and the hybrid is most steady. I'm not sure he likes the rides as much as I do.

Today for him, it's just too hot.

I take my bike through the trail to the park, do a loop around Ring Road, then head to the Outer Harbor. It's at least fifteen miles, going one way. I have nothing pressing.

I've drunk three of my water bottles already and when I see an ice cream truck, I stop to buy more water.

One bottle? I say.

Two bottles? I say.

How about three?

I drink them all right away.

I approach the bridge again, go up and around. And down, to the Ship Canal Commons. The bathrooms are closed because of COVID. I stop behind a bush to pee.

On my usual bench, I hear the song of birds. I hear the hum of traffic. I feel the heat pound on my skin and it reminds me of my childhood on the farm, being in the fields, picking stones and baling. Milking cows, mowing the lawn, dropping hay down to feed the heifers.

STATS

I still wait to hear back from the state about my license. I can't reach anyone by phone. No one's answering my emails.

Today clouds like eyebrows move through the sky and hide behind trees.

It's my triathlon club's open water swim night. When I get to the point, it starts to rain. Thunder. Some of my fellow team members are already in the water.

I stand and watch with others who, like me, question being out in lightning.

We stay tuned to the radars.

When the weather clears, we decide to don our wetsuits.

We dive. We swim. We roll.

SING WITH THE BIRDS

I move my arms and legs against the waves. Boats are in the water now, some kayaks.

Signs here say: No fishing.

People fish in the corner end. Signs also say: No swimming.

But my club has a permit that our president applied for before COVID.

Waves crash in my face. I have a safety buoy. Some fellow club members stand at the sidelines with binoculars to watch us.

Some of my fellow members pass, ask if I'm OK.

I rest on my buoy. Thumbs up. All is fine here.

After I reach the pier, I lift myself and head to shore.

Enough for me, I say to the ones waiting, to the ones done before me.

At shore, we talk about the status of the current. Muscles. Fuel. My body feels OK.

It's not like swimming in the pool.

This lake is an animal.

QUINTANA ROO

In his truck, the man offers me his ice cubes. They're in a tall cup in the console. He says, There's no alcohol in there. It was just iced tea.

I say, Alcohol might help now.

He says, Maybe a few shots?

I can't do shots. I'm OK with wine though.

We make small talk as I wipe the blood from my knees, my fingers, my arm and shoulder. He's given me his t-shirt. He says it's clean. He says he's from the island, has lived here his whole life.

I don't normally get in trucks with strange men. At least, not anymore. I start to wonder if he's single. He looks probably my age, perhaps a little older. After I came to, after my bike crash, I saw him standing over.

He looks like the high school sweetheart I reunited with ten years ago, a month after my dad died.

I was still in shock then.

Tonight's another time trial. When I drove into the lot, I saw our club photographer and told her I had new pedals on my bike. Going back to the clips. Tonight I'm on my tri bike: Quintana Roo. I can clip my shoes into the pedals and that helps me go faster. We talked about past spills and she said, Let's not talk about spills now. She took some pictures and I started on the ride.

And it felt spectacular: all along the water. The Niagara River. Nearing on a full moon and a pretty marvelous sunset, I passed some of my peeps: them going their directions, me going mine.

I rode two miles one way, unclipped my shoes, turned around and clipped again and then went nine miles the other, turned around there, and went nine miles back. The wind was against me at certain places, but I felt strong. High. At one point my Garmin told me I was going 24 MPH. I felt good and steady. The course is flat.

After sixteen miles, at the final turnaround, I tried unclipping my shoes. But I wasn't fast enough and I wound up on the pavement.

I at least had the sense to turn off my Garmin.

I saw the man standing over me. He said, Are you OK?

I remember his lashes. The sea of his eyes. Blue.

I got up. I felt fine. I had goals. I wanted to impress myself. I wanted to impress my friends. I wanted to rise into the sky and sing a hallelujah.

I said, I have two miles left. I need to get back and break my time. My friends are waiting for me too. They have a first aid kit.

Are you sure? he said.

I saw you fall, he said.

My truck's over there, he said.

I can give you a ride, he said.

You don't look so good, he said.

Your shoulder's raw, he said.

I can bring you back to your friends, he said.

I'm good, I said. I have to get back to them. I'm on a time trial.

After he walked away and I tried to get back on my bike, I realized I was shaking.

We make small talk in his truck. I gobble up his ice cubes.

After he brings me back to my friends, I hold onto his t-shirt.

My triathlon friends say things to me like: You're going to hurt tomorrow. This will screw up your suntan. Your shoulder looks like steak. Here's some ice. Here's some wine. Here's some paper towels. Here's a chair. Where's our first aid kit? We're sorry. Can we help you?

The next morning, I roll out of bed. Hardly standing up straight. I am slow to take the dogs out. I take them to the yard. There will be no walking.

It's July 3rd and tomorrow is a Saturday. So today is a holiday—my clinic is closed. I drive to the ER, where I stay for seven hours, have a CT and ex-rays, bloodwork. Scans show broken ribs. I have contusions and road rash on my arms and legs and fingers—most likely a concussion.

I still have this man's shirt. He gave me his name. I try to remember.

THE MAN WHO HELPED ME

My apartment's still so hot. I finally shut the windows. It's hotter to keep them open, which lets in the heat and the noise of motorbikes blaring off the Interstate. And the bus: loud even in its rule-following, letting people off and on and off...

I use SkyMiles to get myself and the dogs a hotel with AC.

We're on the 12th floor. I look down into the city and out to the great lake—where I ride along it on the bike path. I look out to the breakwall.

The dogs tilt their heads. I tell them: I could've found a better hotel, but not every hotel likes you.

On the bed, I sprawl the best I can.

I turn up the AC.

I go to Walgreens for the third time since my crash. Buy more dressings. I'm getting to know which kinds work better for the road rash on my knuckles, my fingers, my elbow, knee. The raw skin on my shoulder.

I take off my old dressings. The bruise on my hip has turned a lighter purple.

I run the shower and feel the water with my fingers. The sting.
I step in, adjust the temp. I address my wounds.
It's my goal to find the man who helped me.

FULL FORCE

Tonight, we're in Niagara Falls, my dogs and me.

It's another option with my SkyMiles. With COVID still in force, it's not like we'll be on a plane soon.

At the hotel check-in, a sign says people from other states must quarantine before coming. There's a wide gap and a shield between the person checking us in and my dogs and me. The attendant's friendly. We all wear masks.

This hotel is only a twenty-minute drive from where I live now.

I go to the 19th floor and look down and see into Canada. I aim my phone camera at an angle. I see the whoosh and whirl.

I put an offer on a house yesterday and it was accepted.

I've been looking, though I took a break after the bike crash. The market is on fire now.

It's a Cape Cod style house in a nice neighborhood. Pretty. Modest. Quiet.

There's gumwood and hardwood, perennials in the yard, a solid firm foundation, big windows, lots of light. Sunroom.

I walk with the dogs. The Falls fall and continue to fall, full force—COVID will not stop them. One winter it was frozen.

It's cool here, a break from the wave.

THE PRODUCE SECTION

The microgreens I buy from the Farmer's Market are so pretty, I want to laminate them and put them in a painting.

They're varied, topped with orange and purple flowers that the vendor says are edible.

It's my first time here this season. I used to come every Saturday before moving in with Henry. The dogs are with me.

I see some of the same vendors. The vegan place, which sells homemade "burgers" and falafel. The Place makes a potent coffee. Some local wineries stay present in their tents, with lines of bottles on their tables, little cups for samples.

Vendors line only one side of the Parkway, spaced very far apart, with sticks and lines and directions saying: Enter here. Exit here. Stand here. Wait in line, please. Signs remind us to wear masks.

Mine steams up my glasses. Pip stops to poop, so I reach in my pocket to retrieve a bag, and I move sideways to pick it up, since my left side is still healing. Happy looks around, his tail wagging and he looks like he's smiling.

I find a trash bin. Drop the bag.

My head hurts. I really want some coffee. My elbow and shoulder and knee and knuckles itch.

At The Place, I ask for a large coffee. Black. Paying cash that I pull from my pocket. I try to negotiate my mask, my dogs, my wounded parts, my bag, and I move my mask when I take a sip of coffee.

At the next vendor, I see one of the first people I met when I moved to this city. I used to date his friend. Last I heard, the friend moved back to London.

I ask him for arugula and chard. When I ask him how he is, he says, None of us are great here.

ROMEO

I agree to meet Don at an Italian place called Romeo.

He friended me on Facebook. We have some mutual friends.

He's been messaging. Telling me good morning. Good morning is an easy thing to say. I can say it to the grocer, to a neighbor. To my dog. To my other dog. To my ceiling.

He owns a remodeling business. He's a handyman. He's also a mountain biker. He's just returned from a trip where he skipped over logs and rode along steep cliffs. His arms are lean.

I figure Don is harmless.

His eyes are green. His skin glows.

WELCOME TO THE NEIGHBORHOOD

Welcome to the neighborhood. Welcome to the neighborhood. Welcome to the neighborhood! I hear as I take my dogs walking in my new neighborhood.

The lawns are manicured, and the homes look pretty lovely. My real estate agent tells me this neighborhood houses lots of cops and teachers. Her son used to play with another boy down the street. I see Biden/Harris signs in one lawn. Trump signs in the next. In another, Black Lives Matter. In a another: No Matter Your Beliefs, I'm Glad You're My Neighbor.

My street runs off another street which runs off of a busier street, and my home sits on a curve in the road.

Like most, my house comes with history—my next-door neighbor told me she knew the original owners: they used to have a greenhouse. There are stone paths in my backyard. Piles, placed strategically. A pergola supports a trumpet vine. The yard needs some work, but I look forward to the spring, when I can plant things and discover.

My art is on the walls. I buy hardware from Home Depot, fix the daybed. Buy some furniture from an acquaintance who is moving. I sign up for Verizon Fios, have the furnace guy come to do a check. Buy a washer and dryer. Order a new piece of art of a woman swimming, one that matches two of my other pieces. I buy a new TV. A smart one.

Welcome to the neighborhood! A man and woman who live two houses down bring cookies with their masks on. They ask if it's just me.

Yes, I say. And my two dogs here.

They leave a card and include their number. They say, We're here if you need us.

I call the security place, same one I used when I had my house built, and I start to wonder if I need it. I call the fence place to get a quote about finishing up the one side of the yard. I call a lawn guy to get the yard cleaned up for this season and sign a contract for future snow removal.

I call to have the fireplace inspected. Buy some firewood. I buy a wreath to put on the door.

I'm set with my utilities. Garbage. Water. Address changes. Voting.

My bikes sit in my second garage, which will fit at least three cars.

Inside, I have two desks. One's built-in, in the kitchen. The other sits in the dining room because it's too big to fit through my doors. I take my computer to my sofa, where I teach. We are still remote and the fall semester is in force now.

I write, using a prompt called Welcome to the neighborhood.

MORE LIKE A MEANDER

On our bikes, Don says, We'll go to Rails to Trails, then Shoreline. Then to Hot Momma's for a bite. Then we'll hit the Scajaquada Trail, through Delaware Park, then to Rails to Trails again. It's twenty miles.

I did the route the day before by myself without stopping.

OH, CANADA

On another ride with Don, we sit at a bench along the river. We watch the sun set on the water, the land on the other side of it.

Far off a bonfire lights up someone's yard; we hear the Beastie Boys.

As we sip beer and talk, the sun gets more orange, shrinking into the land, and the clouds grow pink and purple, reflecting on the water. The music far off turns to something softer.

I get up and lean along the railing.

Don comes up behind me, puts his arms around me. Kissing and touching and kissing and touching.

JUMPS AND TRICKS

Don flirts with the waitress a little. When he asks if that's OK, I ask him what he thinks.

LIKE A PLANET

My massage therapist twists my body on the table. He says, Pretend you're applesauce.

His name is Sal; he's lean with dark hair and, without his mask, I see his five o'clock shadow.

He's about my son's age.

He asks about my home projects. His hands are on my abdomen. He's working on my pelvis. His voice is gentle.

He bought his house two months before I closed on mine. His is on Grand Island. He owns some land there, is living in a trailer because he's gutting out the house and doing everything over.

As he moves his fingers, I tell him about my sugar maple. Huge. It's like a planet.

He pulls on my legs, swings me across the table.

It's rotting, I say. I'm having it removed next week. Probably on Thursday.

He says, What about the wood?

As he presses on my feet, I say, It's going through the grinder.

He says, I can take it. It might save you some money. I'm a carpenter. I can make you a table.

He's from Spain. I hear his accent.

He takes his socks off. He presses his heels into a section of my back that needs some pressing into.

CARRY ON

Don and I get takeout. He sits at my dinner table across from me and eats his meatballs. I have eggplant. He tells me about his weekend camping—his mountain bike pals, and I tell him about my adventures with the girlfriends from my triathlon club: Kit and

Mary and Kay; we hiked, we ate, we ran. I mountain biked on a ski slope south of where I lived with Henry. Don's ride was yet more south. He knows Henry. He doesn't know my girlfriends. Don and I talk for hours on the sofa. The dogs sit at our feet. We move around the house some.

HE DOES TRICKS

The morning's crisp yet wet from recent rain. Some tree leaves are still green, some yellow. The ones on my sugar maple that's going down are orange and red.

My friend Greg—the bike mechanic at the shop where Henry works—texts me; Henry's getting yelled at by the boss for standing around watching.

Greg comes over and helps me load firewood from another friend I know from the campus restaurant—we put tarps in our cars: his Ford and the back of my Mercedes. We go up and down stairs wearing gloves and my other friend provides us with small talk.

Greg and I unload the wood in my garage, then go on a long bike ride to a classy little place on the water.

He talks about his ride in Colorado, where he once rode over two-hundred miles in one day in the mountains. He took a few dives on a few occasions, busted up some bones, bruising up some organs.

We ride our bikes back to my house and he teaches me wheelies.

I DARE YOU

Don's going mountain biking with his pals again today. We've been texting. He's all worked up. He says, I'm coming over.

I text back, I dare you.

The maple branches wave to me. The tree has such strong roots. I wonder if the animals will miss it. I wonder if the ground will.

THERE'S A LADY SWIMMING IN THE POOL WITH HER MASK ON

And she swims lap after lap after lap.

THE CURVE OF THE ROADS

I ride almost fifty miles with my girlfriends—Kit and Kay and Mary—over hills like mountains. After we get to Mary's chalet, we talk about the ride, the wind, scared we would blow over.

We gather wood and make a fire and talk about the close call with the fallen tree, the swerve. We drink beer and wine and we talk about the triathlon season. The pandemic. We hope the races won't be cancelled.

THE TALLEST ONE ON SOUTHWOOD

A team comes out with tractors and risers. A man high up with a chainsaw cuts off a branch of red and orange and yellow. It's sad to see the sugar maple fall. I stand across the street at some points, taking pictures.

I feel sorry for the tree. It was the tallest one on Southwood.

My massage therapist, Sal, who took some of the tree's wood shows me patterns of its insides. The core of it is dead. There's some growth around it from when the previous owner tried to save it. It's an interesting pattern. It'll make a decent table.

Now all that's left of the tree's place is a big wide hole. I'll have to fill it, probably come spring. I'll plant another tree, but the arborist advises me to plant at least a few feet from it. Maybe a Rose of Sharon. Something ornamental.

Still, with that tree gone, the raking is exhausting. It left a lot of leaves. And the back yard is leaf-covered. There's an oak and countless other small ones.

A man comes by and says he grew up a few houses down. He asks about the tree.

The original owners of my home were horticulturalists. They were like grandparents to him. He shares old pictures—a gardener's dream, with rocks and beds and all kinds of colors, patterns.

Birds dance and sing. Squirrels hop from branch to branch, their tales flopping. They sit with their mouths and front paws working on the acorns.

I rake. I rake and rake. I get new eyeglasses and I'm not sure the prescription is right because the leaves make me dizzy.

I put leaves on a tarp. I fold and lift it and pull it to the curb. I leave the arrangement in a rectangle.

MORE FUN THAN I IMAGINE

I tell Don he owes me a date.

I'm not a drama queen. But I have needs, I tell him.

HANDS FREE

I watch Don sleep. I like to watch his chest rise. He's snoring though, so I move into the guestroom. When I wake, he's gone.

I text him, What happened?

He texts hours later to say he thought I was sick of him.

TRIATHLETE

I hire a coach.

I feel the strength growing in my arms and legs and core. I meet Mary at the aquatic center and a man in yellow briefs who was an Olympian gives us advice on form. On the deck of the pool, with our masks on, we practice arm strokes. Mary, who I call MermaidMary, used to do the doggie paddle. She calls me SwellElle.

Kit has contracted COVID. She's a nurse and gets tested every week. She still runs every day. I leave a care package on her doorstep, with wine, and behind the door she's drinking a red one. She has to quarantine.

I buy a leaf blower to try to get my leaves under control, but it's noisy and doesn't work right. I return it and buy another but I can't get that one to work right either.

The leaves continue to fall. Like the COVID cases rise. My county is back in the orange zone, so the local pool is closing. But the county over's still in a yellow zone, and I'm a member of the Y, so I can go to that one.

FIREWOOD

It's time to bring the plants in from the sunroom.

On the first snowy day, I bring in wood from the garage.

I make a stack in the fireplace. I start the fire with my lighter. I watch it spark and spread, turning red and pink and purple.

I sit with Pip and Happy on the sofa.

I say, What have we made here?

BLACK ROCK

Don and I sit on rocks along the river. Across, we see an intersection: a streetlight and cars. That is Canada. We're on Unity Island, not far from the apartment where I lived after leaving Henry.

We ride to another path one block from my last apartment. It's a secluded wooded area with discarded tires and beds and doors. Dirty clothes. The trail is elevated, parallel to tracks. Graffiti covers walls of abandoned buildings. He says, some buildings are being made into apartments. We bushwhack our way through certain spots, go over hills, through puddles. At another point, I see parts I've never seen. Don gives me history lessons about what the city was like before the 1800s. I ask him how he knows this.

Down, on one side of the hill is a parking lot, where a man services his car with the hood up. Kids run around, and I hear laughter.

We look up at a tree, spare without its leaves. Don points to a nest.

A train finally passes.

WE'RE STILL HAVING FUN

I talk to my heart when I run. I hear the dum-dum drum drum feel of my feet on the cinder. I come to run at the park because the softer feel of the surface is kinder.

Kit says that swimming is like sleeping. You just move. It's boring.

I love to sleep. Sleeping is lazy. If I can look at running like sleep, and being lazy, then I shall embrace my elevated heart rate.

TAKE IT EASY

My physical therapist says, on a tele-visit, the pain in my leg is probably my hamstring. It only bothers me while running.

After Kit's recovery from COVID, she drives over in her van and removes her bike and we ride. She says she should probably take it easy.

It's windy. On one of the curves, the wind pushes me into her. She veers away from me, and I end up falling on the pavement.

I'm wearing a lot of clothing. Cushion.

After a few hours, we ride back to my place, where I offer her a beer, then two, then three, and her biking pants collect a lot of dog hair.

I pull up my pantleg and a part of me is bleeding.

LONGER THAN I'VE BEEN ANYTHIING

I sign up for a Half Ironman. I follow my coach's instructions. I do workouts like assignments—make my body do its homework.

I go back to my physical therapist's office, surprised that it's still open.

Masked, after he checks my body, I warm up on the stationary bike. I do squats and lunges and twists. I pretend it is a dance. Strengthening my hamstring. At the end of our one-hour session, he gives me written instructions of things to do with my body until he can see me again three days from now on Thursday.

UNITY ISLAND

Hear the parade? I say to Don and Kit. We ride our bikes out to the tracks and I listen for the choo.

We're on fat bikes. Kit has mine, I have one of Don's and he's on the one he calls b1 (Beautiful One).

It's winter. We have hats and gloves on.

We stop at the 7-Eleven. Kit goes in with him while I watch the bikes. She comes out with a six-pack of the blueberry beer we like. Don's got IPA.

We ride over another bridge, back to Unity Island.
Today the rocks seem slippery. Today we will stay off them.

SCULLING DRILLS

If you google pain cave, you get all kinds of descriptions. Sufferable. Torture. Self-sabotage.

Pain cave to me is about bringing up the heart rate. Bathing in the elevated state and the love of feeling so alive.

I think of these things while living in my pain cave: a room in my house with a treadmill, elliptical, bike trainer. I swim at the aquatics center (finally open again!). My Garmin shows my progress. I study variations of my heart rates. How fast I am. Or slow.

My coach assigns me a threshold workout: swim. Sculling drills, some kicks, and a bunch of freestyle. I feel my body, my arms, the whole core of me moving forward, breathing hard. I'm a fish in a puddle.

BIRTHDAY GIRL

Don comes over, but he doesn't stay long. Gin leaves a package at my door. One of her girls has contracted COVID—she hasn't seen my new house yet—I text her, thank her, and say once things settle, maybe we can have a girls' night and I can treat her for helping me move. My former neighbor Fay also leaves a package. I get texts from John, from Mary, Kit and Kay. Nice calls from my son, my mom, my sister. I finally put my grades in.

I work out on my trainer, take a bath, sing myself a Happy Birthday.

RELAXING THE EGO

Don comes over all dressed up.

Before he arrives, I ask how he wants me: naked or with clothing?

He requests a skirt or possibly some sweatpants.

I opt for a sleeveless dress I bought some time ago at the weeklong workshop about relaxing the ego.

His daughter has a birthday. After seeing me, he's meeting his ex-wife and kids for dinner.

He lets himself in. Opens my fridge. Finds a beer.

I have a fire going.

Well, he says. He kisses my neck. He kisses my shoulder. He tickles my skin and breathes into my soft parts.

SPARKLY ONE

Kit takes my fat bike again, since it's a better fit, I take Don's sparkly one, and he's on his Beautiful One. We layer our attire, add extra clothes to the panniers. It's the eighteenth of December.

We ride the Rails to Trails, then go to the off roads, by the tracks. We get maybe fifteen miles in when we come upon a set-up made of tents and some kind of rigged system used for heat and cooking. There are canned goods, clothes hanging, lots of boxes maybe used as blankets.

Kit says, This person is resourceful.

We find more underground places, along railroad tracks and abandoned buildings. On a rocky downhill, I get a flat. We don't have extra tubes and want to ride more, so Don suggests we ride back to his house—it's just a couple miles, and he can fix it.

Then he gets a loose pedal. My flat is getting flatter. We need to keep moving to keep warm.

I say, I wish I could run. I'm wearing hiking boots and not running because of my hamstring.

Kit says, I can run.

I ride on my bike. Still wearing her helmet, Kit runs. Don rides with one pedal while pulling along the bike with a flat. We're on the main roads now. People stop to ask if we're in trouble.

We're fine! we say.

We're professionals.

We laugh.

We say, This is crazy.

HELLO?

Don calls.

I'm emotionally unavailable, he says.

I say, What do you mean?

He says, I'll never be your boyfriend.

I say, Did I ever say you would be?

THE BIG SPLASH OF ME

I meet MermaidMary at the pool. She's sorry about Don. She says I don't deserve it.

I say, Some of this is my fault.

Kit arrives and swims in the next lane. She says Don is fun, but that's probably all.

I swim, feeling my body, rotating my core, cutting through. I like the sound of my breathing out, the water, the sound of my movements: my legs kicking, my arms reaching: the big splash of me.

On a video call, my hypnotherapist takes me on a journey to my childhood, where, in the sky, after church one night, I was sure I saw a fairy.

My massage therapist, Sal, uses oils on me, pressing his hands on some points, releasing my contractions.

My physical therapist grabs my leg, moves it around, and stretches.

When I hear the train hoo-hoo-hooing on its tracks, I think of Don.

I have dreams of being on a skateboard with Henry. He's always ahead of me. He's always leaving me. He's always telling me he can only go so far. I have dreams of my son. He's always still a child. Reaching for me, with his childhood laughter.

I run on my elliptical machine. My heart rate rises. It gets boring and I sweat, resorting to my brain where I pretend my soul can dance. I'm a very competitive tumbler.

AVATAR

Christmas Day, I go for a hike with one of my triathlon friends and two other girls she's invited. It's an open invite for women who'll be alone on Christmas.

The ground is white, the trees like ornaments, and we walk around a lake that isn't quite yet frozen.

We see a woodpecker banging its beak into a tree. Its more visual than audible—the whole world in this realm now seems another planet. The sky is gray. It's like a dystopia, if you compare it with how this park might look in any other season.

I'm a bit high from an early workout on my bike trainer, where I rode for an hour: connecting my updated Smartbike—the one I just had delivered—an app lets me interact with a virtual world: a game with other riders. I ride and sync—a route called Watopia—a fantasy world—while listening to music by Metallica.

I raised my heart rate to 180. It stayed there for an hour. I passed avatars belonging to real bikers on the screen. Winning achievements along the way let me up my avatar's gear: jerseys, shoes and glasses. Even a fancy helmet. One of the riders who kept passing me on the screen had neon tires. One had purple shoes. I figured they had earned them.

RIDE THE HORSE

On a full moon night, I ride solo.
> I imagine a new man with onion eyes, a glitch in his system.
> He invites me to reveal so many of my dark sides.

THE BEST WAY TO GET FASTER

MermaidMary says I should meet her friend, Drew. She shows me his Instagram photo, in only his shorts, which reveals his V cut. He's an Ironman.

In his hand is a banana.

He's 52, like me.

He lives in Rochester. I can get there in an hour.

He's an internal medicine doctor.

Lately Mary and I swim at the university, with a coach.

People come in speedos and swim caps and take control of the water.

I'm one of the slowest. Still, it's a good workout, and the best way to get faster is to swim with the fast ones. I'm still working on my form here.

Drew and I start following each other on Instagram, then Strava. After I send him my number, he texts me right away. He's vegan, like me. Liberal, like me. He asks me to send him pictures, so I do. He sends me pictures, too.

He goes to work wearing PPE. He hasn't had a day off in weeks. He works in a COVID unit. He says he misses having contact.

I have video chats with him in his office. He looks sexy in his blue scrubs. He looks at me so intently, which unsettles me, so I try to fill it up with small talk.

Later he asks for more pictures, then more pictures, then more pictures.

I play along for a while. I tell him to behave. I ask him to be gentle.

TO THE EDGE

At the pool again, I move my arms. At certain points, when I try to concentrate on form, I panic.

My coaches tell me to relax.

My hypnotherapist takes me back to a story about being in a pool in high school with my girlfriend. She—my best—is dead now. We rode our bikes there. She's the friend I went cross-country skiing with. She died in an accident a few years ago. In the pool, we thought we saw a ghost. We kicked and screamed and kicked and screamed and finally got ourselves to the edge and out of the water.

We sprinted at high speeds on our bikes, the slap of the wind on our wet faces.

EMBRACE THE PROCESS

Drew texts me in the morning and asks if we can chat.

I'm still in bed. Of course we can chat.

He has nice muscles, a nice smile that warms me.

I made a point to tell him earlier this week that although I'm kind of playful, I'm not only about play.

He says the only people he sees are his colleagues and patients, behind PPE. He says all they can see are his eyes. He wears a mask and gown, a shield and gloves. Conference rooms have been converted into patient rooms. There are patients who need ICU beds, but the hospital can't find them.

He still trains at night on his bike trainer, using the same app. He runs on his treadmill. He works with the same coach as me.

On the chat, he says he's really sorry.

We can go into our pain cave when we cycle, kicking gears and jamming to the things we like to jam to.

He says he likes me. He appreciates me. He tells me he is suffering.

BACTERIAL GROWTH

We swim at the pool together: Kit, MermaidMary, me.

We run, using our legs.

We cycle miles and miles.

Drew wants pictures of us. I tell him he is crazy.

I FINALLY HEAR FROM THE LAB

I finally get a call from the lab I interviewed with in the early days of COVID.

There's an executive order that waives a New York State license, as long as one has national credentials.

This interview's in person. I have to check in with security. I wear a mask. I wait for the manager who takes me up to a room to meet with another manager.

They want someone with experience. They seem to value me. I want to be a part of something that wants me to be a part of something. There are politics on campus. There are politics everywhere.

I say, I'm still a professor. We're back in session. But all my classes are still remote.

The job is part time. Evenings. I've worked every shift there is.

They take me on a tour: it's all so familiar, though of course now there are upgrades: technology, computers. I take in the smell: petri dishes, chemicals, blood.

It's a place of lab coats, gloves. Microscopes: blood bank, hematology, serology, microbiology. I'll be COVID testing.

The interviewers ask, Do you like to pipette?

I HAD THE SHOTS

I'm offered the job. I have to get a physical.

The job offers healthcare. I have VA healthcare. I also have healthcare through my career as a professor.

I answer the questions on the form. I sit on a chair with my mask, pen in hand, checking boxes.

I'm relatively healthy.

The nurse draws my blood to make sure I'm immune from measles, mumps, rubella. Hepatitis. I've had the shots, though I can't find the records.

The nurse fits me for an N95 mask, pumping an aerosol. She puts a big hood over me, blows the aerosol again. I can't smell anything. She takes the hood off, then puts the mask in a paper bag, and tells me to bring it to work when I start there.

It's nothing like the masks in the gas chamber. In the air force. The tears, the mucus. The rush back into some clean air.

The nurse cuts some samples from my hair to do a drug test.

I have to lie on the table for the doctor to inspect me. Touch the floor. Raise my hands. Bend over.

BEING QUITE FASHIONABLE

I spend a whole afternoon at a shop that sells scrubs.

I buy four different pairs in different colors and styles. I imagine myself in the lab again, being quite fashionable.

At work, we wear masks—I don't need the N95—and gloves and lab coats.

We focus on our instruments. We treat them kindly.

MY JOB IS TO TEST

Machines click and whir. When the processors leave specimens for me in the urgent rack, I get somewhat excited. Not because they're urgent, but because my job is to test the urgent ones, and I'm eager to get these done and out and get the doctors what they need, the nurses what they need, the patients what they need, the families of the patients what they need, to get this virus over with and back to what everyone might need, though what I need now is the urgency of helping those in need, and I realize that's what I miss about the lab: it's not so much my need—most of this job is technical, and numbers. There's a life behind every specimen I place in my hand—and even those I don't, because sometimes specimens get lost, and that's why when I print reports, it's my responsibility to find them.

The COVID vials are colored with red caps. With fluid on the bottom. Swabs still in. I've had more than a few COVID tests myself.

On my first day—my orientation—the manager, in his office, showed me the different swabs. The skinny one goes deep up into the sinus, the fatter one should only go up past the nostril. Some collectors have shoved the fat one up too far. There were some bloody noses. He talked about the inventory crisis: a lack of some reagents, and then the pipettes. How the state provided medium to collection sites, ignorant that the medium is not compatible with the needed chemicals and buffers for testing, causing lab instruments to clog, which not only confuses the machines, but damages them, and wastes so many valuable, expensive and hard-to-get reagents and hard-to-get equipment.

I understand. I work well in a crisis.

The first days during the Gulf War, I watched the big cargo trucks stacked with packed duffel bags take my then-husband away. I worked thirteen, fourteen, fifteen-hour days on the blood collection team—beginning those days by dropping my baby off at daycare and ending them by picking him up again. He wasn't a year yet. I drew blood units from airmen, tested them and spun them in a centrifuge, separating plasma and platelets and storing red cells in a freezer, shipping them to where my then-husband was: to a base in England where I was later sent when he wasn't there anymore, where I learned people were surprised he even had a wife.

One of the instruments I work with is the Panther. COVIDs designated as urgent: Asymptomatic Admissions, Unexpected Labor and Delivery, Symptomatic Associates, Urgent Surgeries, things like that. Once a sample goes on the machine, it takes almost four hours to finish. There's also a Rheonix—for mostly hospital employees, patients with upcoming surgeries—tests that are routine.

There are windows in this lab. I barely even notice. I'm caught up in the testing.

One of our machines is called a WASP. Another is a KIWI. There's also a molecular lab that takes most of the specimens marked non-urgent. That lab can test ninety-four at a time, and sometimes I have to look to them when it comes to finding things on my reports that are pending.

Under the fume hood, I pipette COVID samples into buffering tubes. Sometimes the swabs fall out. Sometimes the fluid is thick and viscous. The tube has to match the patient. I focus on the names.

I wonder, for as long as time affords, about the lives behind them.

STRONG ONES AND WEAK ONES

On a mandatory hospital break, I get out the cheat sheet that gives me the combination to my locker, where I get out my laptop, and sit in the room filled with fridges and microwaves. Tables. Other lab workers gossip about what one person did, a lab result, and someone had a baby.

I find emails from my English professor colleagues debating about a major name change. There are particular voices. There are strong ones and weak ones, and probably some, like me, who think things like this, at this particular time, aren't really that important.

I get my beets from the fridge, and after I put them in the microwave, I check my latest text from Drew. An upside-down smiley face.

I figure: what the hell. I text him back with a cartwheel emoji alongside a very big tongue.

FINE AS ALWAYS

After I clock in and don my lab coat, it's all about the specimens.

The guy from day shift sits at the bench processing tubes.

I say, Hi Stu. How'd the day go?

He wears gloves, his lab jacket. He's probably my son's age.

He says, Fine as always.

I listen to the click and whirl of the machines. Kind of in a rhythm. Like me earlier today, practicing my breaststroke in the pool, my freestyle, then the butterfly. I swam underwater for a while, practicing a dolphin kick. I used to be a pretty good swimmer—could swim underwater for a whole pool length or two, until somehow something scared me.

I feel my fingers in the gloves, wear the mask on my face, and the lab coat warms me.

Stu gives me the low-down—a few urgent COVID tests are pending, the one machine is updated with controls. He asks if I'm willing to give up one of my upcoming shifts. He's a student. He needs the hours.

I wonder about the science of words: RNA and DNA, and oligos and chemiluminescent and amplicon and lyophilized and acridinium ester molecules.

When I read the manuals, I crave to know more. And then I think: what a lovely set of prompt words!

I pipette. Scan tubes, label. Process.

Nearing the end of my shift, one of my co-workers looks out.

She says, Is it snowing?

I say, It's dark. It's hard to see.

She says, Do you mind, for a second, if we turn the lights out?

SAFETY DEVICE

Driving home is a bubble. Me in my car, the snow on the roads and loaded onto people's yards and houses. The bubble in the lab is of another kind, hearing the bumble and hiss and hum of the machines, them beeping when needing maintenance or if something doesn't work right. There are barcodes on samples, thick and thin stripes that register patients' names and info with the required tests, and when the tubes come in from receiving, I separate the inpatients from outs, stats from routines, and then I place them in the proper racks.

As I pipette, I pop the tops off tubes. I need to get to the fluid under swabs, and certain types are stubborn.

At this work, I don't talk about my writing. I don't talk about much to my co-workers about things besides the testing.

I don't want to feel popular. I don't want to be popular.

But since a COVID test is the most popular in the world these days, am I popular in some ways?

HE HASN'T HAD A DAY OFF IN A LONG TIME

In a text, Drew says he's too selfish for a deep connection.

He says he needs a day off.

He's tired and exhausted.

SEVEN HORSES

In the COVID lab, after I ask my co-worker how her weekend was, she says, Pretty awful.

It's hard to read her expression behind her mask. He eyes look red and big behind her glasses.

She says, I had to put my horse down.

Machines click and whirl. Every now and then the phone rings.

I got my second COVID shot and was glad to have only a sore arm. During my last shift four eves ago, my co-worker said she wasn't going to get the vaccine because she was too scared. She was sitting on a chair, doing vaginitis testing and I was putting tubes onto the Panther. I said, I'm more afraid of getting COVID.

She's working with our supervisor on something, so I move to another section of microbiology, to process some nasal swabs for flu: scanning in the barcodes, putting stickers on more tubes, pipetting under the safety hood with gloves on.

She shows me pictures of her horses on her cell phone. She has seven. Cameo's hoof got infected. The horse was twenty-one. She shares pics of the others. Miniatures.

She shows me the pictures of her land. She and her husband have almost twenty acres.

The phone rings, someone checking on a test.

I GAVE IT AN EFFORT

Some nights, after working in the lab, I get home after midnight. My dogs bark and I let them out. I feed them. I try to keep up with my classes, committee work, advising. My home needs a good cleaning. I'm trying to keep up with triathlon training. Some nights, I fall asleep in my scrubs on the sofa.

My COVID job has limits—I'm not allowed to do a lot of the things I used to—though I'm certified nationally, in New York, I'm restricted.

It's just too much.

My boss says I'm welcome to come back. He says he's really sorry.

I say, I am too.

This used to be my life. It's OK, I tell myself. I wanted to be useful.

EVERYONE'S TALKING ABOUT BIRDS NOW

At a nature writing workshop at an institute the year before the pandemic, I confessed I didn't like birds. How they can prey onto a head. Their beaks are pointy and they make weird noises. They seem so unclean.

It's nice to see them in the sky with wings. I like to fly. I like to get on airplanes. Sometimes, when I run, I put my arms out.

But birds can peck away at things, like my paternal grandfather pecked away at my feelings and my innocence when I was tiny, tiny, tiny, and even into my thirteen years.

He was a birdwatcher. Text-book style. He had all kinds of bird books and lived in the woods with his wife, my grandma, who was mouse-like, following him with her arms and hands and legs and her downright posture.

In the moonlight and daylight, and even in my dreams, I live within my cells. My hypnotherapist takes me deep while I nest into my room. Since COVID, we first catch up on Zoom, and then, on phone, after moving to my bedroom, with my eyes closed, she's able to transport me.

She helps me find my angel, with enormous wings, who takes me to fine places. I float on a cloud. Sometimes I resort to the creek on the farm where I grew up, where I used to visit frogs and tadpoles. I go low then high, where I find my spirits. She tells me they are with me. I find my aunt, my uncle, my dad, my one former therapist who jumped out of a high rise. My childhood sweetheart who found himself a handgun.

MY YARD IS A SEA

And then spring comes. A kaleidoscope of colors in my yard, a kaleidoscope of birds singing in the morning. A rainbow of sounds—unlike the hard drum of the icebreaker I heard on the lake early in the winter. The sky was grey then. I wore gloves and wool socks and layers all over my body, my breath pushing into the cold air. I was on my bike with Don and Kit, and I thought it was just a tugboat, with Icebreaker painted on it as a name, and I said, that boat's name is Icebreaker and they said: because it's an icebreaker, and then that became an icebreaker of an icebreaker. I took a picture, with my gloves on, and then we moved along in order to get warm.

It's the end of March and my budding yard is a sea of white and pink and lavender and yellow. Green. Already! I imagine the original owners arranged various colors to appear throughout the seasons. I've never seen so many bright colors so early in a spring. Popping up, without any of my doing. Are their spirits with me? Are their spirits hanging out with my blood spirits in the heavens? Having cocktails, maybe? Flying around with wings helping other spirits?

It's a gift to love.

I can fall in love with most things. A tree doesn't have to love me back, for instance. A flower is just a flower presenting itself.

EXTREME SPORTS

Don calls. He says, Want to ride?

I have a 4.5 hour ride planned—part of my Ironman training that my coach had set up for me. I imagine riding to Niagara Falls.

Don says, How about riding through the city?

We're on road bikes—I'm on the one I bought from Henry. We go south, toward the Outer Harbor. Along the ride, he shows me properties he's flipped.

We ride and stop at his favorite places on the way: bars, where he drinks beer and buys one for me. I should know better. After dark, he rides ahead of me and I crash into a light pole.

I don't know where he is. My bike is totaled. A friend of his takes my bike to his place, but his friend is creepy, telling me how beautiful I am and asking me for my number, so I venture out, and tell him to leave me alone.

My phone is about to die. I call Kit and she gets me an Uber. I take the ride to Don's place. I let myself in. I find his bed, where he's passed out, sleeping.

I wake up. I have to pee.

Back in the bed, he doesn't ask about the bruises on my face, the skin lost, my banged-up knees and shoulder.

We fuck. He's aggressive, rough. He tells me to get dressed so we can retrieve my bike and so he can get me home again.

In his truck, he apologizes about fucking me in ways that may have seemed forceful.

I touch my face.

FIVE THOUSAND TIMES HARDER

I take up boxing and learn to roll with the punches. It's a novelty to me, and I finally get the line now.

In the ring, people teach me. Hit me, says the first one. Five-thousand times harder.

I'm not sure I've ever hit anyone, save my sister as a kid when I punched her in the stomach and felt so bad I cried for days. I'm not sure why I punched her.

The instructor is a champion.

He brings me into the ring and tells me to hold my arms and hands up to my face to protect them. He tells me how to stand, with my left foot, then my right one. He has mitts on his hands. Right, left, hook. He tells me to hit with my fist out. Harder, he says. Harder! I use my all my force, and punch, punch, hook! Into his mitt. He asks for this and I know that he can take it.

There are about twenty boxers here, starting on the hour and we rotate stations with each whistle. I go from a session with the coach to a session with another boxer, and we test each other's limits, then we rotate from one bag to the next: there's a heavy one, a light one. There's a set of tires one can hit. There's a rowing machine, a place to do some ab work.

My friend Alice brought me here. She's 72, in my triathlon club. After she told me she started boxing, I said to her, Bring me?

She teaches me how to wrap my hands.

I look up boxing terms, like washboard and palooka.

I return to the ring, my hands up.

HOW DO YOU LOVE?

I place my fingers in the dirt and ask myself, How do you love?

I love the darlings in my garden. When one flower fades, another brings on new surprises. I take pictures, discover with an app called Picture This, which tells me what a flower and/or weed is. I look further into the etymology of each word, each flower, each bud. I sit in my garden for hours with my gloves on. The scents of lilacs and wild onions. Daffodils, lilies, irises, and roses.

I run, I swim, I ride. I raise my heart rate more than ever and come home to my dogs.

Mike, a man I met in the early days of COVID, talks of flying me somewhere on his plane. He lives in Webster, on the lake, with a beautiful view and an Irish Setter, Tru, whose grandfather was a Westminster champ. Tru is the happiest dog I know, with his big paws and his way of fetching. He licks my legs. When Mike goes to meetings in the morning, Tru and I hang out by the lake. On the bed, he lays on his back. Mike owns his own business. We've had sex at his house a few times, and I've woken up to his big windows, facing the sunrise.

He lives near Drew. I squirrel my way between these two. It's an hour-and-a-half drive for me. Drew and I are back to texting and chatting. We've only seen each other once, on my way to see Mike. Drew was at work at the hospital—we met at the park where we had sex in his Mercedes.

I imagine loving many people. Many plants. Animals. Everything around me.

DREW ONLY STAYS AN HOUR

Drew only stays an hour. He's checking his phone. He says he still has patients.

Mike, the CEO, is a cyclist who doesn't wait for me on the ride. He has to leave on his airplane to negotiate a deal at the last minute. I ask if we'll keep in touch, and because I asked more than once, he said that made him feel unsettled.

We fucked more than once. We fucked more than twice and three times.

He made me lots of coffee.

There's a judge, lots of cyclists, a banker. I've opened up my range.

I remind myself I'm sensible. I'm a professor. A triathlete, with friends.

Mike said to me, when we started talking a year ago—we were mostly off at first for many months because he found someone else—he just wants to fall in love again. After one of my recent visits, he said he told his kids about me. They're grown. This man is in his sixties.

I thought I was starting to fall in love with him when he said he had to get on his plane again. He has not been in touch since he landed two days ago. Or maybe it's been three?

I was a cop once in the air force. I aimed my rifle. I never arrested anyone.

WHAT TO PLANT WHERE

Weeds are everywhere. I stand in my garden with my gloves on. My garden is my playpen. At first, when I saw colors arriving in the spring, I thought I was a rock star. Now I'm like spoon in a bowl full of grapevines. Red raspberry blossoms, Virginia Creeper, buck-thorn, lilacs, lilies, poppies, fleabanes. Weeds and non-weeds. Dirt and stones. Trees and bushes. Fruits and vegetables. Patching up some grass, after last fall's removal of the maple.

Grades are in. The semester is over.

When I lived with Henry, I loved seeing the deer making themselves at home outside our windows. Families of them, resting. Families of them, nuzzling with each other. A doe nursing her fawn twins. Out there, I got fascinated with fungi. Going out and taking pictures. I joined a local mycology club. I learned things from that group, that, by now, I've mostly forgotten.

My next-door neighbor says she used to ask the original owner (who everyone called Buddy) what to plant where, because she knew it all. I have a newspaper article that another neighbor brought over about the garden. My house was one of the first in the neighborhood, modeled after a Cape Cod house featured in a magazine. I have a picture of that house. I have pictures of this house after it was built. I have pictures of the early garden. Buddy and her husband Harry's greenhouse was torn down by the last owner.

Picture This helps. I find so many things they make me dizzy. The app tells me what my plants are, their origins, whether they're invasive, how to care for them, or how to eradicate, if that seems the way to go. I wonder what Buddy would do. I picture her fingers in the dirt. I picture Harry in the basement, in his woodworking studio, the shelves now empty. I even google the late couple—I know they're no longer with us and that they couldn't have children. They handed out candy to the neighborhood kids before that sort of thing started seeming suspect.

I imagine being a child myself. On the farm. Same one where my dad and aunt grew up, and their parents, and then their parents. I used to collect bouquets of violets for my mom and present them to her to try to show how much I loved her. We had lilac bushes by the oil tanks, and I recall the smell of the blooms, climbing on the tanks, the smooth hard surface of them, and the effort of my muscles getting up them. I recall the feel of my body, doing chores, picking stones from the plowed fields and throwing them onto the wagon with my mom and dad and sister, and then later us throwing them onto the stone pile that had been building up over the past century, by my dad's parents, and their parents, and then their parents, too.

In the yard, I find more things. I take inventory in the morning, walking the yard with my camera. I avoid the thick parts with the trees and bushes, not quite knowing yet what's in them.

I spend the day going to the dark parts of my yard, pruning dead branches, ducking to get under them.

CURIO

My aunt had a curio cabinet that was passed on to her. I picture it passing from one home to another, the passing of one woman to the other in the line of the women blood-related to my father. My dad and my mom sold the farm after his breakdown and then my mom divorced him. I used to dream of putting my hands back into the soil of that farm. It's still, even as an adult, my safe imaginary place by the creek, seeing the minnows, putting my feet in. The curio cabinet wasn't just a cabinet. It also included various teacups that my aunt and grandmother and great-grandmother and great-great-grandmother accumulated on their travels. After my aunt died, the cabinet stayed in the house. But after my uncle died, his sister took over the estate, and after I asked about the cabinet, she said my aunt had wanted it to go to my niece, but my niece didn't want it, so she had it sold.

Once, when I was a girl, maybe four or five, my mom had something else to do, so after school, I was supposed to take the school bus to my grandma's. Not my dad's mom, but my mom's. Those grandparents also lived on a farm. I didn't want to go there. I missed my mom. She said there would be a surprise. So, after I was in the house, my grandma gave me a candy bar. A Snickers.

That's no surprise, I said. I know what the surprise is.

I'd been eyeing a flower in yard. It was bright and pink. A poppy.

My grandma said, So, what's the surprise?

I brought her to the poppy.

My aunt's friend emailed me late fall to say she had the cabinet. She said that she'd heard I wanted it and that if I did, to arrange it to be removed by June. I said, Of course I want the cabinet. My uncle's sister had told me it was sold, along with the things in it.

My late aunt's friend said that when I come to get it, to make sure it's wrapped up finely. Or if I have a friend come, to make sure they won't break it.

My son says he doesn't want it. But will he change his mind someday? If maybe he has children?

I know how much my aunt had loved that cabinet and its contents. She and my uncle couldn't have children.

I hire a company to bring the cabinet to me. I learn from my aunt's friend, that it also includes all the items in it. My aunt's friend calls me once the driver arrives to pick up the cabinet. There are papers to sign. There's more to pay, on my end.

It's fun for me to fantasize where the cabinet will go. Imagine myself sipping from my late ancestors' cups, toasting to the late owners of my house and garden. I'm not ready to be anybody's ghost yet.

PINK STREAK

I call my bike Pink Streak. She's pink, of course. Bikes are flying off the shelves since the start of COVID. Bike chains and even non-chains are opening new shops. I call the managers from one store, then the other, to find what I need.

I have eight bikes, and some people say I'm crazy.

Pink Streak is made of carbon, has disc brakes and electronic shifting. Aerobars, and her whole frame is aero and dynamic. I've only had her for a week. I bought a kit to match, and a friend was selling her pink helmet. A Rudy, with Mips, meaning it's meant to protect the brain in the event it needs protecting. I have pink gloves and pink bottles. I wore pink a lot in high school. People said I looked like Molly Ringwald.

I bought Pink Streak from the same shop as my last bike. Henry isn't working there anymore. Greg got me set up, fitted.

I've been training hard. Pink Streak is my reward.

Pink Streak is a Lepidoptera Odonata. A moth appearing in prairies. It's pink. It flies. It's nocturnal.

GENEVA

I arrange for my friend Mary to watch Pip and Happy, and drive to Geneva for an AquaBike. I was signed up for a Half Ironman, but since my hamstring is still sketchy, I switched to the swim and bike.

I have an Airbnb lined up: an RV on the water. A couple hours from home.

It's summer. I have a break from classes.

The race is Musselman. It's the same place as my first triathlon, ever. Eight years ago, after the first time around with Henry.

After I arrive, my hosts give me a tour. It's a cute place with a retro theme: lots of teal and purple. The man says, We have puppies.

Puppies?! Can I see them?

WE ARE ALL SO WET

I look at the buoy ahead. Move my arms, pretend I am a stuntman. That's not helping, though, with all the other bodies around me in their wetsuits and their swim caps. The water makes me rock, and I keep swallowing its water. I sense a sea of unwanted confetti that makes me sick and want to vomit.

I'm supposed to finish in an hour and ten minutes. I can do that in half that time on a good day.

My body goes limp. My head feels like foam. I tread water and I panic. A person comes over in a kayak and asks if I'm OK.

I feel like I can't breathe.

Swimmers pass in their pink and green caps. The lifeguard in the kayak tells me to take in air through my nose. Another boat comes over and gives me a red thing to hold. It's floaty and rectangular, something I see lifeguards holding all the time at the pool I frequent.

I hang on to it and say, If I turn around, can I still do the bike course?

No, says the man.

I've done my share of triathlons. This is my longest swim in the open water.

The waves of the water keep slapping.

I saw Drew at the start. Yesterday was his birthday. He had salt tablets for me. He drove to the RV where I'm staying. I was on my way out.

Five minutes, he said?

I said, I'm nervous about getting my bike to the transition.

He seemed so casual. I got out of my car and went to his open window and he eyed me and told me how good I looked. He gave me a tap on the lips.

No one really cares what time you get there, he said. I saw him at the start. In his wetsuit. He was with his friends. I tapped his shoulder, hugged him, said good luck.

I hold onto a raft, a kayak, and swim from one buoy to the next until I can catch my breath again. I tell myself, Don't get caught up in the storm. Or maybe that's a lifeguard. There are a few others like me struggling.

I have flashbacks of other things happening in water.

When the lifeguards ask me how I am, I say, I've always been an athlete.

They talk me through. From one buoy to the next one.

I do the backstroke, and one guides me with her paddle.

Finally, I see the chute of the swim finish, which will lead to the transition.

Officials in orange shirts at the swim finish yell. They say to me, You got this.

I move my arms and legs and as I near the chute, people in orange shirts cheer and say: You made it!

But they keep saying, 3006: you made it!

My number's 3006, or maybe it's 3003?

I feel so defeated. I do not believe them.

An orange-shirted person standing at the chute extends his hand and pulls me up. I catch my breath. People cheer.

They say, You made it!

My wetsuit is so heavy. My arms and legs are too. I can hardly believe it.

I rise from the water.

As I run towards the transition area to get on my bike, another orange-shirted man says to me, You made it!

I light up and jump. He hugs me and we spin.

PUPPY

The day I bring Pipette home, I place her in a crate in my Mercedes. I bring a stuffed teddy bear with a squeaker in it for her. A bone. A baby blanket. She whines a little.

I say, What's the matter, Little Girl?

V.I.P.

I'm in my hotel room in Wisconsin with my mom the night before Nationals.

I drove here from New York. Took the ferry from Michigan to Manitowoc, Wisconsin. I haven't even had Pipette for a week yet. Pip and Happy are staying with a sitter. They're not crazy about a puppy, but I figure they'll adjust, and who cannot adore her?

Pipette's a GoldenDoodle. Black. She's smaller than Pip and Happy. Pipette is like a mini Pip, though Pipette will outgrow him. I named her myself. She reminds me of a pipette, by the way she shoots and jumps. It might be an odd name, but I can do what I want.

I picked up my mom in Green Bay along the way. At the hotel, after checking in, we unloaded stuff. We set up Pipette's crate right away.

My mom said, Is she going to destroy things?

I had a rolling list of things to do before my race: drop off my bike, pick up my race packet. I purchased VIP passes for my family: my sister and brother-in-law are coming, along with my niece and her new husband—they live in this state—I had so much swag for them that I had to wait until the end and have some help carrying the things out.

When I get back to the room, I lift Pipette and cradle her and kiss her.

I put the race chip around my ankle. I put the tattooed numbers on my arms and legs.

I had to qualify to get here.

I give Pipette a bath in my own shampoo. I go to sleep and wait for the race.

TOO BIG TO FIT ANYWHERE

Longing. Lounging. Lunging. Hating waking up. Biting my fingernails. Finding a gem of a flower in my yard. Holding my puppy. Hugging my puppy. Picking up my puppy's poop. Opening the top drawer in the desk I had refurbished— that's too big to fit anywhere except my dining room—that holds my maternal grandfather's binoculars he wore during the Second World War. Finding his uniform hanging in the closest. Letters he wrote to his friends when he served. Bullets. Army razors. How I took them when I found them and put them in my pocket. He was dead. My grandmother was dead. My uncle was dead. And the farm that had been in the family for years and years and years was going up for auction. The living had to clean it.

There was my grandmother's teacup. She was a farmer who put on her bandana every morning and went out to milk the cows. I never saw her drink tea. I never saw anyone drinking tea on my mother's side of the family.

Will I miss anything when I die? Will I miss wondering? I won't miss wondering if there's anything hereafter.

CRISP WHITE SHIRTS

My paternal grandfather was tall. He wore overalls a lot and wire glasses. On Sundays, when he went to church, he wore crisp white shirts ironed by my grandma, and slick dark slacks. I imagine him in shiny shoes, though I don't remember his shoes much.

I remember his smell, clean like Zest. What I remember mostly is the house where he lived with my grandma. An A-frame in the woods. With a kitchen table that looked down into the trees, where we could watch the birds and squirrels and the deer that frequented. We had devotions at that table, where we prayed to Jesus. We drank coffee—what a luxury for a child—and we dunked our cookies into coffee cups and sucked what we could of the treats before they dropped and melted.

I remember his smell in the bed, when I crawled in with him in the morning. I loved his warm body and raw scent. He'd cuddle with me. I was just a child, and it was a reprieve to be with him after the fear I experienced every day living with my father.

Once, at home, on the farm, a huge turtle sat in the middle of the driveway. It was bigger than me. Our farm, before it was a farm, was a swampland, and I imagine the turtle now, having been there longer than me and any members of my family. My dad was born on that farm. My grandfather was, too. My great-granddad got the farm going after coming over on a ship.

I don't remember what my dad did about the turtle. I just remember it sitting there. It was a very slow-moving creature.

ZOOMIES

At the block sale, kids have lemonade stands, offering drinks for fifty cents. I don't have much to sell—or rather, didn't have time to get much ready—so I opt to walk the block, maybe meet more of my neighbors. I'm told that this neighborhood is friendly. I find that to be true even though people stay in their houses more these days because of COVID.

I wasn't sure if it would be un-neighborly of me to not have stuff in my garage for sale and am relieved to see I'm not the only one. My neighbor across the street the night before said she didn't have time for it either.

I don't really need anything. As I roam the block, I find things I like enough to buy. A set of four wine glasses for a dollar. Rain boots in my size, never used, for twenty. I would have liked to find some bike stuff. Though I probably, if prepared, should have sold some cycling goods of my own.

Pipette is teething. She has zoomies, running in circles, jumping up, trying to bite me. MermaidMary has an older puppy and uses a squirt bottle. I've already tried that. Mary says to try a racquet.

I see one at the block sale. I wear a hat that says DOG MOM. A gift from Fay after I brought home Pipette.

I call her names like Little Girl. Babydoll. Sweetheart. I don't think Pip and Happy are so happy, but I talk to them and tell them that they will be.

I make soup in the kitchen and the puppy jumps. I hold my racquet. I blow my bubblegum and she tries to pop it. I pour cereal and she puts her paws up to the counter. She tries to spike her teeth into my arm, so I wear long sleeves. Sometimes gloves and mittens.

The vet gives her her four-month shots, which means she's in the clear; I can take her to the dog park.

I hang onto my racquet.

She cuddles with me and I hold her, singing the way I did to my son before he became an adult and then a soldier. Swinging him and rocking.

FREESTYLE

The smoke detector is on, I remind myself, swimming laps, focusing on the angle of my elbow. At the pool. Feeling the body of water on my skin, though I don't think about it much these days, now that I've gotten less scared.

The open water's something else. It can surprise you. Take you under. With its waves and undercurrents.

Like the deer that jumped out in front of me on a bike ride.

My twin earlobes, the jam of my head between them.

As I swim, kicking my legs, making sure to rotate my body, angling out my arms, turning my head to breathe, I tell myself my puppy will not jump on the range again, will not start up a burner, turning the gas on, lighting my place on fire with her in it like my friend's dog did last month and left the place and her poor dog in ashes.

I'M AN ANIMAL

I clean the house. Smile at myself in the mirror, not liking anything I see, hoarding bad thoughts, talking to my dogs, saying things like, It's good to know you.

But then I'm up again the next morning, waking on the sofa, with a leafy pillow. Having left the back door open and fixing my eyes to a new toy from Pipette. I put on my glasses.

Pipette sits upright, proud, tongue hanging. And the toy is not a toy, but something that looks recently alive. A squirrel. On my new expensive rug in front of my new expensive puppy.

The thing is plump. With blood. A body and limbs. And eyes. I try not to look any more than I have to.

My puppy is alive. The rug isn't. The squirrel isn't either. I want to make sure, but I don't really want to look again. I kind of scream again a little and go to the garage to find my shovel.

As I lift, I close my eyes and pretend it's a potato.

There are dead leaves all over the backyard. I watch them fall. Let the dogs out. They frolic.

Pipette runs in circles. She has a curly tail, long legs, and the darkest eyes and fur.

She likes to smell things.

Sometimes she just sits, in her regal posture.

She raises her nose. She barks.

Inside, I give her toys. I get on all fours, play with her, and pretend I'm an animal.

ANIMALS IN LIPSTICK

At the dog park, I watch a dog jump into a leaf pile.

The piles are carefully crafted, in sections. The park was closed until two p.m. today so workers could rake. It's a large park. A whole island. Twenty acres.

One dog's owner kicks his own legs in the pile. My puppy approaches the pile, sniffs. I think she wants to play with the dog, though she wants to play with just about any other creature.

I think about jumping into the pile myself, but you never know what's in there. I haven't even raked the leaves in my own yard. I hired a company and am still waiting.

I don't mind the dead leaves, but I mind things that can hide in and around them. I imagine a junkyard of carcasses and skulls. I've seen some in my back yard. I've had dreams of animals in lipstick, licking honey, playing etudes on my piano, making fun of my alarm clock.

These days I sleep downstairs on the sofa that faces out into the sunroom. I see out to the back yard. The back yard is enormous.

I go to the upstairs bathroom, where I spy on Pipette outside, through the window.

She romps around. She does zoomies. Sometimes, she just sits, upright, guided by her nose, her ears, her eyes.

She's curious. She has so much to learn.

HOW DO YOU ROLL?

Things I love about my new home: having a full spread on the bed if I want. Bright colors. Lighting candles. The whir of transit buses passing. Keeping my life clean. Being organized. Being able just to find things. Eating meals at the table. Not always having the TV on. Being close to Wegmans. Cooking for myself. Doing my own laundry. Enjoying my art, my plants, my dogs. Long soaks in the bathtub, taking in my salts, lavender oils, lights down, with a lit candle and low music. Practicing self-care. Knowing where my clothes are. Being able to exercise whenever and in whatever ways I want. Drinking wine with dinner. My nice, big kitchen! Cooking vegan, cooking non-vegan, or not cooking at all. Making my own plate. Not having to hear bad things about liberals. Being liberal. Writing at my desk. Reading. Being quiet. Feeling cleansed.

Asking my dogs: how do you roll? Walks to my favorite park, where I can fly a kite if I want. Being in awe of the enormous sky I can see clearly out my window. The pandemonium it makes when a storm breaks. Making a lime into a kickball. Acting like a whimbrel or a warbler or a goose. Being silly with myself. Playing imaginary golf while playing an imaginary trumpet, eating imaginary (or real) blueberry sherbet in my fluffy velvet robe. Oh, how scrumptious!

My place smells so delicious! Can you study my serology? Can you tell that I am free now?

LITTLE GIRL

What's your name, Little Girl? I say to Pipette.
    What's my alibi? I say to Pip, who tilts his head when I speak.
    What's the matter? I say to Happy, who hides under the sofa.
    I have faux fur blankets on the beds and on the sofas. Waterproof covers to protect my furniture from accidents and paws. I wear thick socks that rise above my ankles. Pipette likes to chew and bite. She eats papers if I leave them.

On the TV, I find dog movies/shows on Netflix. *Benji* and *Beethoven*. Dogs bark and run on the big screen. Pipette sits, watching, intent. Happy comes out from under, and Pip doesn't care. He is mostly catlike.

Pipette's five months old and forty pounds now. I start making homemade dog food. I find recipes. Add supplements.

I trade in my Mercedes for something more practical. Bigger. The two small dogs have their own seats in the back and Pipette is in the front, strapped in with her seatbelt.

When I was a kid, I dreamt of a large family.

My hypnotherapist takes me to my childhood. We travel to high places, low ones, then I hang out in the clouds, where I find floating flowers, fairies, dogs with wings, and I rest on the body of an angel. I place my fingers to my thumbs. I'm a deva. Full of magic. Peace. I belong here. I am home.